THE SHADOW DRAGON:

ORBS OF FIRE

May you live your dreams!

5-24-15

By: Amanda Schmidt

COVER ART BY:

AMANDA SCHMIDT

For my children, family, and friends who believed that I was more than I thought I could be.

TABLE OF CONTENTS

CHAPTER ONE

"You're too slow!" Marty yelled, scowling at me before he turned to the rest of the team. "And she was faster than the rest of you by a hundred yards!"

All the guys groaned, and I could feel their eyes boring into me. I glared at Marty, who ignored me. He seemed to find great pleasure in turning the team against me, which wasn't hard since they were irritated that I was more than capable of being the best.

Marty didn't care that I was better than any of the men in the area or that I could lead him to a triumphant year at the Tournament. He was not happy I was female, he did not like that I was better than the others, he despised that I would not quit, he hated that I was here, and he was not afraid to remind me as often as possible.

The world was changing from the old ways, but it did not mean that everyone was accepting the change. The only reason Marty was allowing me to be here was because of his brother, Alex.

Six months ago, Alex had brought me before Marty to ask him to train me. Marty had argued vehemently with Alex, and I was certain that I was going back home. The whole team and I watched as

1

Alex and Marty walked away from us. It didn't take long for all the boys to start making derogatory comments about why I was there, but I wasn't listening to them. I was too busy trying to hear what Alex and Marty were saying to pay attention to them.

I had already defied my father by coming here, and having to go home was unthinkable. Unfortunately, it sounded like that was exactly what Marty was planning to do. The argument was not too long, but long enough that we were all sure that I was headed back home. However, Alex got his way in the end and here I am.

When Alex and Marty interacted, I was never sure if Alex was the younger or older brother. All I knew was Alex came across much wiser. Alex and Marty looked the same age, but that was where the similarities ended.

The best I could guess, Alex was about ten years older than me. Alex had a powerful aura about him that most people found intimidating. I thought this was ridiculous because Alex had a compassionate nature that set him apart from everyone else. Especially Marty, who was closed-minded, mean, and hot-tempered.

I didn't know Marty as well as Alex, but I knew he was nothing like Alex. Alex did not see the world in black and white like his brother. In fact, when Alex talked I could see a rainbow of colors that opened my eyes to a world of possibilities. Whereas Marty saw everything one way and if you dared to argue with him he would make you pay dearly.

2

I had no ties to Marty, nor did my father. Before Alex left me here I had only seen Marty a few times during the Tournaments - at a distance. This probably only added to the friction between Marty and I. It was always a male swordsman from *his* team that won the Tournaments, and now there was me – a female swordsman, who was better than everyone else. And to make it worse, his brother discovered my talent, not him.

As much as I wished someone else could train me, Alex had entrusted me to Marty. Therefore, I had to believe that Marty's tactics were going to improve my abilities. Although most days I was certain that Marty was trying to make me give up.

Alex, on the other hand, had befriended my father years ago. We were on the verge of losing our land when he had ventured into our lives with perfect timing. He not only talked Lord Vertas out of slaying my father in front of me and my sister, but he stayed with us to help my father work the land. Within a year, my father had made his debts right.

My father was so thankful he opened our house to Alex for the rest of his life. He even offered my beautiful sister, Krissy, to him. Alex politely refused, saying that it was not in his blood to be tied down. For which Krissy was overwhelmingly grateful - for she was secretly seeing someone else. I often wondered if Alex had known that. He never seemed to miss anything.

"Sonia!" Marty yelled in my ear, startling me. "Since you think that you are so much better than

3

everyone else here, why don't you make a run through the Batwas Valley."

I heard the laughs as I turned my attention to Marty in disbelief to see him smirking at me. Marty wasn't quite as tall as Alex, nor were his shoulders as broad, and his hair was red. His brown eyes did not carry the same wisdom as Alex's. Marty's eyes had a cruel look in them - a look that always put me on the defensive. I squared my shoulders and met his stare, nodding confidently.

"Hold on," he said slyly as I turned towards the valley. "Leave the weapon, it is not yours."

I didn't even glimpse at him this time. I quickly removed the sword that was sheathed on my back, and dropped it on the ground. This time there wasn't laughter, only silence.

"If you're not back in four days, I will inform your father that you will not be competing," he informed me.

I bit my tongue and stared at the Batwas Valley. One of these days…

"You might want to start running. You'll want to be well beyond the middle before it gets dark."

I couldn't miss the mocking tone in his voice. He knew he was sending me to my death, but I was going to prove him wrong. I didn't know how I was going to do it, but I was going to return in less than four days. As I started to run towards the valley, Marty began yelling at the others that they had four days to beat my best time. I highly doubted that they would be able to.

4

I smiled at the knowledge that the next four days would be the most frustrating for Marty because I was better than any of his boys. None of those guys had ever even come close to my average time. My smile vanished as I thought about there being a very good chance that I would not return to see the outcome, no matter how badly I wanted to prove Marty wrong.

It was said that the Batwas Valley ran along the Ancient's realm and was home to creatures that this land had only ever heard of. Stories had been told of people who tried to find this realm, but no man or woman has ever returned from that adventure. No one knew if they were killed before they made it there. Or if they did reach the Ancient's realm, was it the Guardians or the Ancients that destroyed them?

The Guardians are the mythical dragons of the Ancients. They are *mythical* because it has been several generations since anyone reported that they had seen them. The legends of the Guardians have practically disappeared, and no one is sure if they ever really existed. The fact that dragons are no longer seen is a good thing. According to the stories my father had told my sister and me, they were cruel creatures that killed people simply because they could.

I ran down the deep green hill that led into the valley, where I would have a choice of two trails I could take. One trail would lead me around the Batwas Valley, but would take more than a week to return. The other trail, the one that would begin my journey through the valley, led to a river. The river

5

would lead me to the heart of the Batwas Valley – this was the area rumored to be closest to the Ancient's realm.

Of course, I wouldn't actually go to the heart of the Batwas Valley. I planned to cut across the untamed land, and from that point, without a weapon, the chances of survival were not in my favor.

I reached the river without any trouble, which should have been a good thing - but it never was. It seemed that anything that started easy would become difficult by ten-fold before it was finished.

I stepped into the river cautiously and crouched low. I slid my hand into the ice cold water and raised my cupped hand to my lips. I drank the ice cold refreshing water as I stared into the forest where few had survived.

The distance of the trail could be covered in a day or less. However, the forest that filled the Batwas Valley was old and many trees have fallen. Not to mention, the rumored creatures living in there that kept most everyone away.

I stared at the trail that continued into the woods. It appeared to be lightly used, and I was confident it would not be long before the trail became nonexistent, making the journey at least a two day run – if I finished. Once I finished, I could run the safer, but longer ridge home that would put me a few miles away from where I began.

I took a deep breath as I glanced around. I knew I had better get moving because it was already late in the day. The creatures that everything feared moved in the night – or so it was said. I swallowed the rising fear and started running, knowing that the sooner I passed the mid-point the better.

Running the valley turned out to be an amazing adventure. The air smelled exhilarating, filling me with excitement. I was hurdling over logs and ducking under branches, running down the winding path that was quickly disappearing. I smiled as my adrenaline pushed me faster. If it weren't for what I feared was coming in the night, I probably would have enjoyed the punishment that Marty had given me.

The darkness came quickly in the valley and the temperature was dropping dramatically. I could feel the cold wrapping itself around my sweaty body. It was unfair for Marty to send me in here without a weapon or the proper attire. I should have swallowed my pride and refused, but I didn't want to look weak in front of anyone.

When it became difficult to see, I climbed into a tree, knowing the ground would become a very dangerous place. I situated myself in the branches, keeping my eyes on the ground and ears open to all the sounds around me. I wrapped my arms around myself, trying to keep my body from shivering.

The night brought the sounds of a variety of creatures that I was unfamiliar with. Luckily, none of them seemed to find interest in me. I continued to sit in the tree shaking uncontrollably, hoping my luck would hold up and I would survive the night. I could hear Alex saying that my definition of being strong seemed an awful lot like stupidity, and right now I would have to agree with him.

7

It was a couple of hours before the forest became silent - except for a sound that sent fear through my entire body. Some of the howls were closer to the tree I was sitting in than I wanted, but one had come close enough to cause my heart to pound in my chest. I focused on the area where the sound had come from. The ground was dark, but the creature was darker. I heard the territorial hiss of what could only be the Ortal. It was too close to the tree I was hiding in. I held my breath as I saw its white eyes pierce the darkness near the base of the tree.

Unfortunately for me, it must have picked up my scent. I only saw the one, but I knew it wasn't alone because they traveled in packs. I was trying not to freak out, because the one thing that had stayed consistent in the stories I had heard were that the Ortal despised trespassers. Alex had once told me about his encounter with them, making him the only person I knew that had seen the Ortal and lived.

He told me they preferred to walk on all fours, but they were more than capable of standing, which would bring their height up to a minimum of six feet. They were known to use their arms of solid muscle to rip their adversaries into pieces. He had shown me a scar to prove to me they weren't just all muscle, but they were also intelligent and had a strategist's mindset.

I continued to watch the Ortal as it circled the tree. My body relaxed a little as the Ortal abruptly began to head in the direction that I had come from as though it caught sight of something far more interesting than my scent. There should have been more of them following it. Where were the others? I looked back at the base of the tree, searching for more white eyes.

Perhaps that one had strayed, and was now catching up with the others. I had only searched a few moments when I heard rustling in the branches above me. I stopped breathing as I glanced up. Drool was clinging to the razor sharp teeth of the Ortal a foot over my head. Alex had said that the teeth weren't what you had to fear, but there wasn't anything to stop the terror inside me from rising.

It let out a low, deep growl, and my brain kicked back on. I quickly dropped to the branch below the one I was sitting on, and continued to climb out of the tree without a second glance. I hit the ground running in the opposite direction I had come. I jumped onto a fallen tree, and used it to hurdle over the boulder that was in my way. I landed in a shallow river and kept moving. My eyes searching for something I could use as a weapon. The water was frigid and my ankles began to hurt, but I knew that the river was the only thing slowing the Ortal down – giving me a chance to live a little longer.

Finally, I saw a fallen tree with broken branches strewn all around. I didn't have to glimpse behind me to know that they were catching up, I could hear the splashes and howls not far behind me, and I fought to keep my fear from consuming me. I jumped out of the river and ran to the tree, snagging a broken limb off of the ground. It was fairly thick, and I wrapped both of my hands around it holding it like a sword.

I turned towards the river to see seven Ortal step into the moonlight, forming a semi-circle in front of me. Even on all fours they were bigger than I had imagined. Their dark skin was sleek, and I couldn't stop myself from noticing that their claws easily cut into the hard ground. I took a couple steps back, knowing that if the tree was behind me, then the Ortal couldn't be.

One of the Ortal stepped forward and began to speak in its strange language. He was huge, and his lean body was covered in scars. I didn't even want to wonder what could have caused the wounds on him. I held my thick stick up, and slanted it in front of me. I took a deep breath, knowing that I was dead if any of them got near me.

The one in front of me made a noise that sounded oddly like laughter. He spoke again, tilting his head to the side, his white eyes never leaving my face. He must be the Alpha, the leader. Alex had said that the Alpha was the most dangerous, most intelligent, and the cruelest of the pack.

It barked, and the Ortal to its right jumped towards me. I swung my stick without hesitation. I made contact with its head, and watched it fall to the ground. There was more *laughter* as a whine escaped the one I hit. I couldn't believe that I had knocked it to the ground. I stared in disbelief before I noticed that all the other Ortal's attention was on the fallen one and off of me. I took that moment to run again.

I jumped onto the fallen tree behind me, leaping to the ground on the other side a moment later. I sprinted through the brush as fast as I could, ducking and maneuvering myself through the bushes and trees that seemed to be getting closer together.

I halted suddenly in horror. I stared at the tall trees that surrounded me in the distance, shaking my head. I was in a clearing, but it wasn't the exit of the valley. I just killed myself.

I had managed to run the wrong way, taking me deeper into the valley. The trees on the other side of the clearing were at least a quarter mile away. The bright moonlight that had aided me in maneuvering through the darkness, now gave me nowhere to hide.

I quickly turned to run back into the trees, knowing that was my best chance for survival. However, the Alpha was standing in the moonlight sneering at me and the pack was standing a short distance away in front of the trees, blocking my escape. The Alpha barked again and another Ortal charged at me. I swung the stick I was holding tightly in my hands, and this one hit the ground too.

I glanced up, hoping that their eyes would be somewhere else again, but they weren't. The Alpha was now walking slowly towards me. I started walking backwards away from him, trying hard to calm my breathing. I was exhausted and scared, but I didn't want him to know that.

He stopped a few feet in front of me, and began sniffing the air. He stood on his back feet, straightening his back. He stood much taller than six feet, and his muscles bulged against his dark skin. I

11

forced myself to swallow. He was still sniffing the air. His eyes abruptly looked into mine, and he bared his teeth at me. He barked again, and this time they all leapt forward. As I turned to run, I fell to the ground. I closed my eyes, and braced for the terror to begin.

When it did not come, I opened my eyes and saw a wall of blackness in front of me. Two Ortal suddenly appeared on the ground. They were not moving and were covered in a shiny substance. Ferocious snarls filled the night but were immediately drowned out by a roar like none I had ever heard, echoing all around and sending terror through me. I tried to see what it was that I was going to be up against, but I couldn't see anything in front of me, except blackness.

I had to get out of here! I turned, but before I could start running I realized that I could see the area in front of me all the way to the trees in the distance. I glanced over my shoulder to see the darkness that was there. I didn't care about what was going on at the moment. I knew I needed to escape the creatures of the valley before they remembered I was here and killed me.

I ran for the trees in the distance that I could see the moonlight shining upon. I only made it about a hundred yards before I had to stop. The Alpha bared his teeth at me and, without a sound, he lunged at me. I raised my stick and swung. He caught it with his hand, which had four inch claws on each of his three fingers. I stared at his claws, claws that were dripping with a shimmering substance that smelled like... blood?

I looked from the claws to his face in horror. He smiled, showing his sharp pointed teeth. He yanked the stick closer to him, pulling me with it. He breathed in deep before he threw the stick that I was clinging to through the air. My body hit the ground hard, and the stick fell out of my hands.

A second later, I was screaming at the horrific pain, resulting from massive pressure on my left leg. I reached for my leg and saw that the Ortal had bit into my shin. I shook my head in denial at the reality that his mighty jaws had crushed the bone. There was no way that I would be able to run now! How was I going to escape?!

The Ortal stood over me, wiping my blood off his mouth. A wave of nausea was quickly washed away by panic, which had scattered my thoughts so that I couldn't figure out what I was going to do. The Alpha dropped to all fours as he spoke quickly. I had no idea what he was saying, but I knew it couldn't be good. I shook my head, I didn't want to die.

I watched in terror as it began reaching for my chest. I stopped breathing and my mind seized with fear as the darkness began swelling behind the Alpha. The Ortal shrieked in horror as its body was lifted and then consumed by the darkness. The Ortal was afraid of the darkness?! This was not good.

I attempted to get up, but my leg wouldn't bear any weight and I fell back to the ground, screaming in pain. There was another roar that echoed all

13

around, sending chills down my spine. I immediately attempted to drag myself away, but the Alpha appeared in front of me again, covered in blood. He grabbed my wrist without hesitating, and began dragging me across the rugged ground as it ran.

I screamed as his claws ripped into my skin. My blood was racing down my arm as the Alpha continued to pull my body behind him. He stopped abruptly, quickly changing directions. The ground continued to beat against my body as it ran until finally my mind overrode the fear and pain. I began to watch the ground for something I could grab and get myself free from his grip. I did not want to die!

After three attempts, I snagged a large rock off the ground. I knew it would be a wasted effort to throw the rock at the Ortal, but with a lot of focus I was able to slam the rock against its hand. The Alpha let go of me and I began dragging myself away, hoping that the Ortal would continue to run away from darkness it was afraid of.

I screamed in agony as the Alpha dug its claws into my left shoulder, lifting my torso off the ground and whirling me around. Horror continued to fill my mind. The Alpha had placed me between him and the darkness that had been chasing the Ortal. The darkness roared fiercely, causing more fear to race through me, fear that made my nightmares seem like childish dreams.

What is that?!

Two orbs of fire suddenly appeared in front of me. A gust of overly warm, moist air rushed against my body. The Ortal quickly grabbed my side, forcing me to scream again as its claws ripped into my flesh before lifting my body over its head.

The thing in front of us growled warningly, and to my surprise the Ortal talked without irritation. There was a pause before he spoke again. The Alpha continued to speak with long pauses until the darkness let out a long guttural growl. The Ortal slowly released my body, and I crumpled to the ground. I wanted to drag myself away, but I lacked the ability. My newest wounds were throbbing and my leg was useless. I attempted to roll over, only to cry out as my whole body protested with pain.

The orbs of fire moved close to me before disappearing into the darkness.

CHAPTER TWO

The light was shining brightly through my window and I sighed with relief. It was just a dream. I wonder if that meant practice was going to be a nightmare. The Tournament was only three months away, and Marty was going to be a monster. I guess I better get up before…

I breathed in deeply as pain ripped through my shoulder, and a duller pain began to throb in my ribs. Panic raced through my mind as I continued to attempt to sit up until a gentle hand restrained me.

"Is she awake?" Krissy exclaimed from across the room.

I was home?! No, I couldn't be home! I began to glimpse over my shoulder to see who was restraining me.

"I think your father is in the fields," Alex calmly commented. "Would you mind going to get him?"

Alex was here? He wasn't supposed to be here. He told me he was leaving after he made sure Marty would train me and would try to be back for the Tournament.

I listened to Krissy walk over to my bedside. She knelt down next to my bed and smiled at me with relief. She carefully swept my hair away from my face.

"I am so glad that you are okay," she whispered and kissed my forehead.

I smiled back the best I could. I didn't feel happy at all. She shifted her attention passed me and smiled at Alex before hastily leaving the room. After she ran passed the window, Alex stood in front of me placing a chair down. He sat down, staring at me with a gentle smile.

"You gave us all quite a scare," Alex said kindly. "What were you doing out there so unprepared? I thought I taught you better than that."

"Marty," I said quieter than I meant to.

I thought I saw anger rise into his eyes, but it left so quickly I wasn't sure.

"Marty…?" he inquired, and I knew he wanted to know *what* Marty had done.

"Told me to run the…"

"You beat his boys again?"

I nodded, "You know how happy it makes him when someone beats any of his *warriors,* let alone the whole team."

"I'm sorry," he apologized genuinely.

I smiled at him. "There's no reason for you to be sorry. I'm the one who wants to win the Tournament."

"I shouldn't have put you on the team and left."

Part of me wanted to agree, but the overpowering part was angry that he didn't think I could take care of myself. "I can handle my own…"

"Yes, I see," he said sarcastically as his fingers skimmed over my shoulder.

17

I tried to swallow the pain, but I knew he wasn't fooled.

"When Krissy gets back I'll have her change the bandages," he informed me with a smile, but he wasn't really happy. "Next time someone tells you to do something suicidal, I hope you'll use that mouth of yours."

I hated disappointing Alex more than I disliked disappointing my father.

"Cheer up," Alex said suddenly as he ran the back of his fingers down my cheek. "You are still young, and the fact that you survived speaks very highly of you."

The memories of the valley flooded my mind and I quickly shifted my eyes to Alex as I relived the fear. "There was something in there!" I exclaimed in a panic.

"Yes, Ortal," he calmly said, "I saw their tracks and blood all over the place. How did you…"

"The Ortal were killed by…by… I don't know. By black… and there were two floating orbs of fire…" I tried to explain, staring at his empathetic face.

I stopped talking, suddenly feeling stupid. I couldn't believe I just told him that. He's going to think I'm crazy. Not that he'd be the first person to suspect such a thing. I closed my eyes, just wanting him to go away.

Alex was the only one who ever understood me, and I was sure I couldn't handle him thinking I was…

"So… You didn't take on the pack of Ortal?" he inquired curiously.

"No, it wasn't me. Marty sent me in without a sword…"

"He WHAT?!" he roared, startling me. I opened my eyes to see that he was moving around the bed.

"You're leaving?" my father asked. "Did Sonia offend you?"

"No, no," Alex quickly answered. "Krissy, change her bandages again, okay? I have to attend to something. I'll be back a little later, Jack. Don't ask her too many questions, she is still pretty weak," he added empathetically.

I listened to the outside door shut as Krissy stood in front of the chair that Alex had been sitting in.

"Father, I have to change her bandages," Krissy sternly said as she focused across the room.

"I think being her father allows me to be in here," he replied.

She glared at him for a moment before turning her attention back to me. Father sat in the chair that Alex had been in as Krissy moved towards my leg. She pulled the blanket off the leg that ebbed with pain. I breathed in as she moved my leg and carefully started unwrapping the bandages. I quickly bit back the pain that was intensifying, not wanting to show that it was really starting to hurt.

"You sure are lucky that Alex came by when he did," my father commented. I shifted my eyes away from the leg that Krissy was attending to and focused on my father. "Although, I wish he would have come by a lot sooner - you were two breaths away from death."

"This is healing wonderfully," Krissy said in surprise, but I couldn't imagine that it was. "I wish I knew what Alex used on your leg. I was sure that you'd never be able to walk properly again, but I'd say your chances are looking up."

"Now, I guess I owe Alex more of my life," our father teased as Krissy slowly rolled me onto my back.

"I'm sorry," I apologized through a forced breath. I closed my eyes against the pain that was almost too much.

"I'm just glad that you're still alive."

I opened my eyes to see that his face was as sad as his voice, and I knew he meant it. We lost my mother when I was young, and he constantly reminded me that I looked like her. She had been on the outskirts of our land when she vanished. His heart broke that day, and I was sure he'd die if anything happened to me or Krissy. We were all he had left of her.

"If you're going to insist on staying, Father, you can at least help me," Krissy said as she finished changing the bandage on my side. "I have to do her shoulder."

I could tell by the tone of her voice that she was not looking forward to this part. My father immediately cringed, and my stomach dropped - there were few things that made Father cringe.

They slowly and carefully sat me up. I held my breath against the cries of agony as pain ran through my entire body until they had finished leaning my good shoulder against Father. Krissy began to unwrap my shoulder, and a burning sensation began to seep into my flesh. I breathed in deeply, which caused more pain in my ribs and tears to escape my eyes. I quickly wiped my wet cheeks on my father's shirt.

"You would think after a week it would look better," Krissy commented as she finished getting the bandage off. "Everything else at least looks like its healing. Do you know where Alex left that cream? I think she needs another dose of it."

"I think it's... I'll go get it," he quickly said. "That is if you think you can sit up on your own," he whispered to me, concern filling his voice.

"You had better run, or I'm going to do more than sit up," I said with a smile.

He carefully leaned my body away from his, and waited to see if I could stay that way. He started to leave, but paused in the door way.

"Why don't you give your sister the good news, Krissy," he said over his shoulder.

"Good news?" I inquired.

She plopped down in front of me with the biggest smile, and held her hand up.

"Kirk asked Father a few days after Alex took you to training, and he asked me the next day!" she exclaimed with a smile.

I stared at the ring on her finger. It was a brown sparkling jewel surrounded by a silver metal. I didn't really care for Kirk, but Krissy was too excited not to be happy for her. I smiled with excitement, "Congratulations!"

"We were going to get married after you won the Tournament, but…"

"Oh… I don't think…" I said, trying not to show my disappointment that suddenly began crushing me at the realization that I would not be able to compete this year. I would have to wait until the next Tournament, which might not be for another five years.

The winner of the Tournament received riches to take care of his land and then some. The winner also received a special gift from Lord Vertas, which was different every Tournament. However, none of these reasons were why I wanted to participate.

The Tournament for me was an obsession - one that I didn't really understand. I only knew that it was what I wanted to do. It was the only thing that mattered to me. I had planned to give the money to Father so that he would never again have to be in the predicament that Alex had found him in. And I didn't care what gift Lord Vertas was going to give the winner this year - there was nothing I wanted, except to win.

"Alex seemed to think that you might still have a chance to compete…" Krissy quickly remarked, but she must have been just saying that to make me feel better. My left shoulder was totally useless, there was no way that I would heal and be prepared for the Tournament.

"We are not going to talk about that right now," Father interrupted as he entered the room.

"Father, he even offered to train her."

"He has already done more than he needed to for this family. We will not ask anymore of him," he sternly informed us.

Krissy reached for the container that Father held, and to both of our surprise he did not hand it to her.

"I'll put it on," he told us.

I glimpsed down at my shoulder for the first time, and groaned with disgust as I quickly focused on not vomiting. My shoulder was horribly discolored and there was pus leaking out of the gouges from the claws that had dug into me. I closed my eyes to hide the tears. I was never going to use this arm again let alone hold a sword.

"Alex was able to get all the poison out of your ribs, but unfortunately, not your shoulder. This is what he is using to fight the Ortal venom," he informed me. "He was hoping that your shoulder would heal before you woke up... he made reference that you were lucky to be unconscious. So, this may hurt."

I glanced up at his worried expression and nodded that I understood. I knew that if Alex thought that it was going to hurt, then it was going to be extremely painful. I clenched my teeth, waiting for him to apply it.

"You should probably lay on your side," he finally said, and I shifted my attention back to him wondering why.

Krissy helped me lay onto my side, and after a few minutes the throbbing in my ribs disappeared

Amanda Schmidt

completely. I screamed into my pillow feeling as though someone had lit a fire in my shoulder.

CHAPTER THREE

I woke up on my side, facing the window. I stared at the sunlight that was coming in. My shoulder still ached, but at least it wasn't on fire. I could hear Krissy laughing outside, and I started to think that Kirk was over until I heard Alex's voice.

Alex and Krissy... talking? No, it was worse than that. She was laughing, and not just laughing, but giggling *flirtatiously*. She and Alex hardly ever interacted. What was going on? I tried to focus on what they were talking about when I heard a ruckus ensue.

"You are not welcome here!" my father yelled.

Was he talking to Alex? Alex was always welcomed here. Did something happen that I didn't know about? I had been gone a long time, and Alex had returned here sooner than he had told me he would, but...

"Easy there, Jack. I came here to speak with Alex," Marty said calmly, and my entire body tensed. I wanted to give that man a piece of my mind.

"Send a messenger," Father growled, and I knew that Alex told Father what Marty had done. I attempted to get up, but the aches in my body kept me down, and I let out an annoyed sigh.

"I will walk you back up the trail, Marty," Alex said, not sounding happy to see him either. "I'll be back shortly, Jack. I would like to take a look at Sonia."

"Of course," Father said politely, but I could still hear his anger.

Everyone remained silent, and I wanted to know what was going on.

"Is Kirk coming over for dinner?" Father asked.

They must have been so quiet because they were watching Alex and Marty leave. I wish Alex had run his sword through Marty, but I knew Alex wouldn't do that, especially to his brother.

"Can he?!" Krissy exclaimed eagerly.

I clenched my jaw at the thought. I could do without seeing him. Although, I guess it was possible that I wouldn't, since I couldn't get up on my own.

"Yes, why don't you go and fetch him," Father replied calmly.

Krissy didn't answer, but I heard her run towards the stable, and shortly after a horse galloped passed my window. A few moments later Father walked into my room.

"I am so sorry," he said sadly as his hand rested on my arm.

I placed my hand on his to comfort him, it wasn't his fault.

"You're awake!" he said in happy surprise.

I began to roll over so that I could see him, but stopped as soon as I started. The aching in my ribs

26

was hard to ignore, but I held my breath and tried again.

"NO!" my father loudly said, causing me to stop my efforts.

Now what? "What's wrong?" I asked, trying to hide my concern.

"Wait for Alex to return," he replied. "He doesn't want anything to touch your shoulder until he gets a look at it."

He walked around my bed, carrying the chair from yesterday. He sat down, staring at me with a forlorn expression.

"What are you sorry for, Father?" I inquired. "I'm the one who should have told Marty to shove it.

"Everything," he answered.

"Father, you have nothing to apologize for. I shouldn't have…"

"You have too much of your mother in you," he smiled. "She was very spirited. She also refused to allow others to make her feel inadequate. She probably would have done the same thing."

"I'm not spirited, Father. Look at me, I'm…"

"You've got a strong enough spirit for this whole town."

I smiled at his compliment.

"Alex told me that there were five Ortal dead on the ground…"

"Father, I didn't…"

"But you fought against them. Most *men* would have never made it two steps…"

"I…"

"If I wouldn't have told Alex to leave, if I would have let him train you, you would have killed them," he said.

"Told Alex to leave?" I said hesitantly. Why would he…

"I had to leave, Jack. It was not your fault. We both know it."

I watched my father glance over my body with eyes that said it *was* his fault. Before I could collect my thoughts, my father stood and moved out of my line of sight with his head down, not saying a word.

"Where's Krissy?" Alex asked after I heard the bedroom door close.

"I heard Father tell her to go get Kirk for dinner," I said slowly, wondering what was going on.

"He did?" he replied curiously and a little disappointed.

"Are you sorry that you didn't take father up on his offer all those years ago?" I inquired, thinking about how they had been alone together earlier, and how Krissy was acting. There was a strange feeling of anger budding in my mind.

"No," he laughed and my anger dissipated. "I needed her to take your bandages off. I want to make sure everything is healing properly."

"I'm going to check the fields, Alex," Father said as he walked passed my window towards the fields. "Do whatever you need to."

He was leaving Alex in the room with me, the door closed, and alone?!

"Jack," Alex quickly called out my window, but there was no answer. He moved to the window and looked out as though searching for him. Alex slowly turned back towards me, appearing to be a little uncomfortable.

"What's with Father?" I asked Alex.

"He's been doing a lot of thinking the last few weeks."

"Few weeks?! Krissy said it had been a week!" Panic rushed through me. How could it be a few weeks?!

"That was a couple of weeks ago."

NO! That couldn't be right. How...

"The Ortal venom had progressed deeper into you than I was aware of. It was good that your father had put that cream on you when he did. The good news is that now all your wounds are healing perfectly."

"Except my shoulder," I stated.

"Well, we'll take a look... Do you mind if I don't wait for your sister? She's usually gone half a day when she goes to *get* Kirk," he said, clearly disapproving of my sister's actions.

"Ummm... Well, I guess if Father doesn't mind, then I don't," I hesitantly replied. "Father helped Krissy the other day. I mean a few weeks ago..." I corrected myself. It really bothered me that I have been stuck in bed instead of training. "And you are Father's friend, almost family. I could *imagine* that you're a father...sort of..." Not really.

"Me, a father?" he laughed, staring at me like I was crazy.

"I mean you've kind of helped raise me. Or...encouraged me to grow like a father...should?"

29

I replied, stumbling over an answer that would make it sound like we should be comfortable in this situation, but failing miserably.

He continued to stare at me humorously.

"Okay, you'd have been a horrible father."

"Horrible?" he repeated, faking that I hurt his feelings.

"For Krissy. I mean, I've turned out pretty good," I stated with a smile.

"You're right: horrible. Look at you, and you think you've turned out pretty good," he said smiling, shaking his head. "I would never pass for a father."

"Okay, how about big brother then, just so you can change the bandages and it won't bother us," I smiled.

He nodded that he agreed, and walked back around the bed. I closed my eyes, wishing I'd wake up anywhere except here. My mattress shifted, and my eyes shot back open with the knowledge that Alex was on my bed behind me. There was no amount of imagination that would make any of this ok. Alex's fingers moved along my shoulder as he gently removed the wrap.

"That is much better," he said as he skimmed his fingers over the gouges. He gently grabbed my wrist, and carefully began to lift my arm. It ached, but not as badly as I expected. It was when he started to move my arm backwards that I breathed in deeply.

"It's not weakness to show pain, especially in this instance," he informed me in his kind voice. "Did it hurt before I started to pull it backwards?"

"It ached," I said honestly.

"Just ached?" he inquired, sounding like he wasn't sure that he believed me.

"Just ached," I assured him.

"I think we will leave the bandages off then. Where are your clothes?" he asked as he got off the bed. "If you continue facing the window, I'll stay behind you, and we should be fine."

"Okay," I said, smiling at how uncomfortable he sounded at his own idea. "My clothes are in the dresser without the mirror."

I listened to him walk over to the other side of the room as I stared out the window, wondering why my father allowed Alex to be in here alone with me. Maybe, he thought of Alex as a big brother figure... not likely. I could still hear my father yelling incredulously at Alex for the things Alex allowed - and usually encouraged - me to do.

His fingers slid between the mattress and my side, bringing my attention back to him here and me just wearing a blanket. He lifted my torso into a sitting position, and I held tightly to the blanket.

His fingers skimmed along my back as he pulled my shirt down my torso. I quickly slid my good arm through my sleeve, but my other arm...

"Umm... Alex, this shirt isn't going to work," I informed him. "There isn't enough room for me to maneuver my arm into the sleeve."

31

"Your father got rid of all your bigger shirts after I told him that Marty had sent you into the Batwas Valley alone. He was going on about how you were going to be more like your sister if it was the last thing he'd do.

"I don't think one of his shirts would do you much good. He's not wide enough and your sister, well, you could try one of her dresses…"

He stopped talking as I whipped my head around, glaring my extreme dislike of just the idea of wearing one of Krissy's dresses. He started laughing, "Okay, no."

His expression became abruptly serious and pulled his shirt off, "This will work."

I stared at him like he was insane, and shook my head.

"What, it doesn't smell… that bad. Okay, I'll grab a different shirt."

He turned and left the room. As he was leaving, I continued to watch him over my shoulder, taking in the details of his bare back. He had several thick scars and a black dragon tattoo with orange eyes on his shoulder blade.

A dragon? Could that have been what I saw? That was impossible, but then… so was the fact that I was still alive.

I closed my eyes and thought about the orbs of fire. The more I thought about them the brighter they became. I could almost see the life within them. A dragon's eyes? But, according to the stories, dragons didn't…

A burning sensation began to pulse inside of me and I became dizzy as though I had been spinning for far too long. The sensations disappeared as suddenly as they started, but everything felt...weird.

I opened my eyes to see Alex standing in the doorway. He had put his shirt back on, and was holding another that was folded neatly. He was looking at me differently than normal, but I wasn't sure what it was that made it different.

"Are you okay?" he softly asked, sounding concerned.

"I was just thinking... nevermind," I replied, shifting my attention back to the window. I couldn't remember what I was thinking about. I put my right hand on the side of my head, something didn't feel right.

"This shirt is clean," he said, and I glanced over at him. He smiled, but I could see that his mind was somewhere else.

"I think I'm going to need some help again to get out of this shirt," I said, wishing I didn't *need* his help. However, there was no way I was going to be able to maneuver myself out of this shirt without it.

"Uhh... okay," he tensely said. He got back on the bed and kneeled behind me.

I stuck my good arm out and he grabbed the sleeve so I could pull my hand out. He grabbed the bottom of my shirt and carefully pulled it up over my head.

Is that his heat I was feeling on my bare back?

He pulled his clean shirt over my head, and I felt his fingers burn intensely down my sides as he pulled

33

the shirt down to cover my torso. Desire enveloped me, and I turned my head to see his face close to mine.

"Thank you," I softly said, and the feeling dissipated.

I quickly focused in front of me. What just happened? I shook my head, and slid my good arm in one sleeve. I slowly moved my left arm into the other sleeve, feeling the pain tear into my shoulder. I clenched my jaw against the pain until it subsided.

His shirt was very roomy. I glimpsed down at myself, the neck line of his shirt hung low on my flat chest. I lifted my hands that were lost in the sleeves and I laughed.

"I look like a little kid!"

"Well you are," he replied with humor. He moved in front of me and rolled the sleeves up.

I scrunched my nose at him, "I'm almost twenty-six."

"Like I said," he smiled.

"Yea, and you're *so* much older than I," I sarcastically replied.

"Okay, let's swing your legs off the bed, and see if they can hold your weight," he quickly said.

He gently wrapped his hands around my ankles, and carefully pulled them off the bed. He slowly bent my knees, letting them rest against the side of the bed. I glimpsed down at my legs to see a jagged mark on my left shin that began just above my ankle and stopped a couple of inches from my knee. I instantly remembered the pain, and the Ortal standing over me with my blood dripping off its face.

I swallowed hard as I touched the mark, and thought about the darkness that had grown behind the Ortal. I could feel my fears...

I quickly glanced up to see Alex's outstretched hand, and I glanced up at his patient eyes. I placed my hand on his, and slid off the bed so that my feet were on the floor. Using his hand, I pulled myself up onto my feet. I stumbled to the side, and his other hand grabbed my hip to balance me. Again desire surged into me.

"Sorry," I whispered, focusing on his chest as he released my hip.

"How does your leg feel?" he asked, redirecting my attention away from his closeness, and the desire disappeared.

"Surprisingly good," I replied, focusing on my leg. It shouldn't have been able to hold my weight. How was that possible?

"Okay, let's try walking," he said in a parental tone. I thought about our earlier discussion and I wanted to laugh.

He put my hand on the inside of his elbow, and I took the first step. My leg ached with stiffness, but that was the only thing I could complain about. It took a few minutes for me to walk across the room, and I couldn't stop myself from laughing.

"What are you laughing about," he inquired curiously.

"That I was at the top of the team, the fastest competitor – lithe and agile. And it just took me how many minutes to walk across the room?"

"I don't really see how that is funny, but I am glad that you are laughing," he smiled.

I glanced down and saw that the hem of his shirt laid across the middle of my thighs. "And you tricked me into wearing a dress!" I said, with fake annoyance.

He laughed as he glanced down at my body. "Hey, can't blame me for trying."

"Krissy will be so jealous that you did it, and not her," I replied as we continued to walk obnoxiously slow. We walked out the front door, and I was almost in hysterics.

"Sonia, what is going on, and WHAT are you wearing?"

I turned my attention to the direction of Krissy's voice, still laughing. "A dress," I said, and attempted to curtsy. Alex moved quickly to keep me from hitting the ground.

"Alex, what…?"

"It's my shirt," he informed her matter-of-factly.

I laughed even harder as her jaw hit the ground. "Ow, ow, ow," I said, trying to stop laughing because it was becoming painful, which just made it worse. "I thought laughter was supposed to be good for you."

I took a deep breath, trying to calm myself. I put my left arm across my stomach to hold my ribs, and felt the pull in my shoulder and I winced.

"Sonia, you need to go back inside," Krissy stated.

She glanced at Kirk apologetically as if she were embarrassed, which annoyed me. She was not my mother, and I could care less what Kirk thought. What was she doing back so soon? Alex said she'd be gone half the day.

"You can go inside, but I'm staying outside. I miss the sun's warmth and the… mmm, wind's caress," I said as the wind blew across me. I closed my eyes to the calming sensation that brought back the giddiness. The wind's caress felt wonderful, and I took in a slow deep breath.

"You've been unconscious," she retorted, and my eyes shot open.

"I still didn't feel it," I said irritably. What was her problem?

"Sonia," Alex said softly. "Maybe, we should go back inside."

"See, even Alex agrees," she said haughtily.

"Krissy, are you going to do everything Kirk tells you to do?" I snapped, feeling my happiness turn into a fierce anger.

"No," she answered hesitantly, her eyes flitted to Alex and I scowled at her.

"Well, Alex isn't my future husband, boyfriend, or person I plan on kissing when no one's paying attention. So, I'm not going to do something just because he wants me to!" I growled loudly.

"Sonia," Alex started in a cautious tone.

I turned my head and glared at him. Did he think I was out of line?! Whatever. I let go of Alex's arm, and hobbled as fast as I could away from all of them. I heard Alex whispering to Krissy, and it made me angrier. Was she interested in Alex? Did he want her?

37

I shook my head. He was Alex, and it was none
of my business. I swallowed the pain that was
steadily growing in my leg, and pushed myself to
walk faster. I could feel the intense burning in my
shoulder, and I put my hand on my sweaty forehead.

CHAPTER FOUR

"Sonia," Alex began as he caught up with me.

"Go away," I growled, letting my hand drop to my side. I was furious that he had sided with Krissy.

"Your mood swings are not a good thing."

I stopped and abruptly turned around, causing Alex to almost run into me. He was standing less than a foot away from me.

"What do want from me?" I sadly said as his eyes locked onto mine. The sadness I suddenly felt was overwhelming.

"I... I..." he stammered, and shifted his eyes the ground.

"That's what I thought!" I snarled furiously. "Nothing. Nobody wants anything to do with me!" I snapped. "Father hates that I look like mother and that she's not here! As if it's my fault! Krissy hates that I'm not feminine like her! That I actually want to take care of myself! Marty hates that I'm better than all of his boys. He wants me out of the Tournament... no he wants me dead! The whole team does! And you, you..." I didn't know, but the thought that I was nothing to *him* shut my brain down.

"Sonia," he said in his kind voice.

39

"Well, I want nothing to do with any of you either!"

"You're shoulder," he said alarmed as he reached out for me.

"Yea, my stupid shoulder is on fire!" I yelled, moving myself away from him. "Because I…" The dizziness returned, and all I could see was two orange orbs floating in the darkness.

"Alex!" I called out in fear.

"I got you," he replied.

"I see orbs of fire," I fearfully said as my hands clung to his shoulders.

"I know," answered an unfamiliar voice, and I tried to see passed the orbs to see Alex's face close to mine.

"What's happening to me?" I inquired, only feeling the overwhelming terror from the night in the Batwas Valley.

"Let's get you back to the house."

"No! Please, I don't want to…" I began in a panic.

"Okay, okay."

"Alex?!" I called, after a few moments of silence.

"I'm still here," he softly said, but continued in a normal voice, "Tell Jack that I'm taking her to the stream, and we'll be late for dinner."

"Who are you talking to?" I worriedly asked.

"Kirk. He and Krissy heard you scream."

"When did I scream?"

I felt the laughter coming around again. "I don't even remember screaming." I shivered as I felt the cool ground beneath me. "You were carrying me?" I laughed. "I'm going crazy, aren't I?"

"No, it's the Ortal's venom. It will pass."

His cold hand moved across my forehead before sliding over my shoulder.

"I was going to be the best the Tournament had ever seen, and now I'm insane."

"Sonia."

His hand touched my face and I focused on his dark eyes.

"I'm going to die, aren't I?" I asked. "No one survives the Ortal."

"Your spirit is strong. You're going to pull through this," he assured me as he quickly shifted his eyes away from mine, his hand sliding over my shoulder again.

Strong spirit? Yea, right. I stared up into the trees above me, when a thought occurred. Why had Alex returned?

"Alex?"

"Yes?"

I shifted my eyes to his face as he wiped his cold hand across my forehead and down the side of my face. I moved my good arm and grabbed his hand before it slid away.

"Why did you show up in the valley?" I curiously asked. Again, my insides were burning for… what?

He stared at me, but didn't say anything. I gazed into his eyes and didn't want to look away.

41

"Did you see the orbs of fire in the darkness?" I asked, trying to ignore whatever was happening inside of me.

His face moved closer to mine. His eyes were so dark, almost black.

"You have all those scars... on your back..." I pointed out, not sure how it was relevant to anything.

His lips were inches from mine. His lips...

"I've seen many battles..." he whispered.

"Are you afraid of me?" I quietly asked.

"No," he breathed.

"You're always leaving, when I feel like our friendship is at its strongest..."

His lips were almost touching mine. His hand slid away from mine, and I could feel the fire underneath his fingertips as his hand continued down the side of my face. He hastily focused on my shoulder, shaking his head.

I closed my eyes. No one would ever want me.

"I will help you get back in shape for the Tournament. We will register you as an independent," he said.

"The Tournament is too close. Look at me! I'm broken, in more ways than one," I stated. I felt like crying, how could things be so terribly wrong.

"You'll be ready," he told me with confidence as his cold hand skimmed across my face. I turned my face into his palm, hoping to not feel the agony in my mind.

"Alex," I whispered, feeling the intensity within me.

"I need to get you home… it's dark, and your father will be worried."

"No, he won't," I said, putting the pieces together. "He's hoping you will take me away."

"It's more complicated than that," Alex quietly replied, picking me up like a child.

"He is giving me to you, and you don't want me," I continued.

"It's not that simple."

"I understood that you didn't want my sister, she had already been messing around with someone and you miss nothing. So what's wrong with me?"

"There is nothing wrong with you, you are amazing. I… I can't take you away from the world you're in."

I turned my head away from him, not believing a word he was saying.

He didn't say anything else as he carried me back to the house and into the kitchen. He carried me to the table and sat me in a chair. The food had been left on the table along with two plates and silverware.

Alex dished out the food and sat across from me. We didn't say anything to each other. I stared at the food in front of me because I didn't want to look at Alex. I couldn't eat, I felt sick.

"You should eat," Alex said after several more minutes of silence.

"I can't," I stated, pushing the plate away and laying the side of my face on the cold table. I wasn't focusing on anything in particular and after a few moments I closed my eyes. I was so pathetic.

I listened to Alex get up, clear the table, he even washed the dishes. He picked me up, and I opened my eyes as he began to carry me towards my room.

"The door is closed," he pointed out.

I rolled my eyes. That was Krissy telling me not to enter.

"You can sleep in my bed, and I'll sleep on the couch."

"Don't be ridiculous," I irritably said. "Put me on the couch..."

He chuckled, and carried me up the stairs.

"Alex, seriously, I'll sleep on the couch. It won't be the first time."

"You need a good night sleep," he smiled as he laid me on the bed. "How's your shoulder?"

I looked away from him, and said nothing. I didn't want to be any more of a burden to him. In fact, I just wanted to disappear and not exist.

"Do you mind if I take a look?"

I didn't look in his direction. I couldn't figure out if I cared or not. He slid his shirt away from my shoulder, and I glanced over at him to see the alarm on his face, but it didn't matter. He moved towards my feet and I bit my lip as his fingers skimmed over my shin, his touch overwhelming my senses.

He put a blanket over me and folded it down to my waist before he lifted the shirt's hem line above the injury on my side. His eyes briefly searched mine, and I saw how concerned he was. As he touched the wound on my shoulder, my desire surged with more intensity than I had ever felt, causing me to sigh.

44

"Sonia, your shoulder... I've not ever seen this before... Sonia?"

He continued to talk to me, but all of me was focused on his touch. It was ecstasy, and I wanted more. He moved away from me, taking the intense desire with him. I tried to collect my thoughts, but my mind was in chaos. I glimpsed over to see where he went, worrying that he had left me all alone. I saw him holding his dagger and tinge of fear slid passed the confusion.

"I think it will be easier if you sit up," he informed me, and after a moment's hesitation I did as he recommended. "I'm going to have to open all the wounds from the Ortal," he began to explain.

He was being very serious, and concern was all over his face. He cut the shirt that I was wearing, and as it fell I shivered at the cold draft that moved across me.

"I'm sorry, but this is going to hurt," he informed me, and I nodded.

I braced myself, but as his hand touched my shoulder again, the intensity took over my brain. I focused on his blade as it cut into my shoulder, watched blood and pus drip down my skin. I didn't feel any pain, just the desires that I was trying to ignore. I watched him skim the blade across the claw marks on my wrist, cut into my side, and slice into my shin.

I wantonly gazed at him. He glanced up at me, but quickly shifted his eyes away from my face, moving his hands away from me. The intensity

45

didn't leave with his hands this time - I could still feel his touch lingering. My body *needed* his touch.

I leaned closer to him, and was pleased that he didn't move away. I hesitantly kissed his shoulder and then his neck. His hand that was not holding the dagger skimmed across my good shoulder and down my arm. His fingers slid along my waist and onto my back, causing fire to pulse in my veins. I moved my lips away from his neck and shifted my eyes to his face. I could see the desire in his eyes. He moved his lips slowly closer to me, his eyes fixed on mine.

He suddenly turned his head and put space between us. As his hand slid away from my back, my desires swung into an extreme rage, and I snagged his dagger from his hand. I swung it at him, cutting his chest.

He stared at me in surprise, but there was no anger in his eyes. I swung again, and he moved away from the bed. I leapt at him and he caught the wrist that held his dagger, twisting my arm until I dropped it. I sunk to the ground in tears as he let go of me.

"Help me, Alex," I begged. "I don't understand…"

A blanket landed gently across my shoulders and Alex immediately picked up my trembling body. He carried me back to the bed, gently laying me down. His arms began to slide away from me and my mind panicked, tears raced down my cheeks.

"Don't leave me, please! I'm so afraid! Alex, what if… What if I don't…"

"Sonia," his soothing voice called. "I'm not leaving you."

"There is so much that is wrong, the Ortal, the darkness... not the darkness, the fire that even the Ortal were afraid of... what if it comes back, what if they... what if I close my eyes and never..."

Alex had laid down next to me, pulling me close to him. "It's going to be okay. I'm here."

I glanced at his face to see he was staring at me, but the concern was gone - it had been replaced with strength. He gazed into my eyes for a long moment, not moving away from me and the panic slowly calmed.

"Sleep," he whispered, and the warm air of his breath caressed my face. His arms held me securely and sleep began to overtake all of me.

CHAPTER FIVE

I sat up in bed, breathing hard. All I could remember was fire and pain. I took in my surroundings, immediately realizing that I was in the guest room with just a blanket covering me. I vaguely remembered what had happened the day before.

I glanced at my left shoulder that was not covered by the blanket. The gouges looked like they had scabbed over, but as I ran my hand over them I didn't feel anything. I moved my arm up until the pain was too much. I had gotten my arm above shoulder level, but it still hurt a great deal to move it behind me. That didn't bother me though, since I didn't need to move my arm behind me to begin training.

I laid my left arm across my stomach as I moved my feet off the bed. As my legs slid out from underneath the blanket I saw that my right shin also had a scab-looking color over the bite mark of the Ortal, making the jagged scar look horrific. The image of the Ortal's bloody face was vivid in my mind, and I waited until I calmed myself before I attempted to stand. As I put weight on my right leg, I was relieved that it wasn't nearly as painful as it looked, and the pain wasn't enough to stop me from training.

I glanced at the chair to see a black shirt folded on it. As I picked it up, I knew it belonged to Alex. Memories of my advances on him slammed into my mind, and I was suddenly very embarrassed. I couldn't believe how badly I had wanted him to want me. Then I remembered the anger and that I had attacked him with his own dagger, slicing him across his chest.

He most definitely had left for good this time. I was both relieved and saddened by that thought. The notion to climb back into the bed sounded like a great idea, but I had a lot of work to do if I was ever going to get in the Tournament on my own.

I struggled to get the shirt over my head with one arm, immediately sliding my good arm in. However, I was instantly irritated at the pain in my shoulder as I put my left arm in the other sleeve. Today was already looking to be another awful day.

I walked very slowly to the stairs, and stared down. I put my hand on the railing before I lowered my left leg to the next step. As I moved my other leg down to the next step, the aching in my left leg became more intense until my right leg joined it and I could shift the majority of my weight onto my uninjured leg. I took a deep breath and continued until I was at the bottom. That was more work than I had anticipated and I found myself fighting off the anxiety that followed at the thought of not being in the Tournament.

I glimpsed at the couch and saw that Alex had already gone. I had hoped to catch him before he left so I could apologize. I was slightly hopeful that, if nothing else, he'd at least help me register for the Tournament.

He must be so angry with me, probably regretting his decision to return sooner than he had planned. My heart sank as I watched my chances at the Tournament slip even further away. I slowly walked toward the kitchen. As I got closer, I heard my father talking angrily.

"You can't be serious!" father said in disbelief. "This conversation is over! I will not let your brother anywhere near her, and he's the only trainer in this end of Lord Vertas's land."

Who was Father so…

"I agree. Marty isn't going to come anywhere near Sonia," Alex replied.

Alex was still here! My excitement quickly faded as my father's words sunk in. He wasn't even going to let me try?

"Jack, you're not listening. *I* will train her and…"

"What?! No! I've already told you! I'm not changing my mind! She can't…"

"It's the only way."

"Absolutely not! She's been through enough already. The Tournament will only…"

"She wants this more than anyone I've ever met," Alex started to explain calmly. "She has so much potential."

It was quiet a moment before my father spoke again, calmer this time, but I could hear the tension in his voice.

"No, I can't let you train my daughter when you've already done so much for me and my family. She doesn't need to be in the Tournament. She..."

"Yes, she does. This is just the beginning. I'm not doing this for you, Jack. Training her is my decision, and I've made it," Alex argued and then paused. "You *know* she needs this training, you've seen how this Tournament has consumed her life. We both know she needs..."

"Then you should..."

"What are you two talking about?" I asked as I entered the kitchen.

They both turned to me with expressions of surprise as they moved away from each other. It wasn't that they were arguing toe to toe, I had seen that often, but it was that Alex had been standing intimidatingly over my father that had caused my interest to peak.

"How *I* am going to train you for the upcoming Tournament," Alex stated, recovering first.

I glanced at my father, who immediately focused on Alex and quickly gave him a nod. My eyes shifted from one to the other suspiciously. They both were trying to act like they hadn't been arguing, and hadn't been in each other's face. Their behavior made me wonder what else they may have been discussing.

"How is your leg feeling?" Alex asked before I could say anything.

51

It was beginning to hurt, but I didn't want to talk about that. I began to walk towards my father, ignoring Alex. My father glanced at Alex again.

"Father?"

"And your shoulder?" Alex inquired as he walked over to me.

"Father?"

"It doesn't matter. Alex is going to train you so that you may do what your heart really wants."

I tilted my head in confusion, I knew fighting in the Tournament was the last thing he wanted me to do. Why was he on Alex's side all of a sudden? I quickly shifted my attention back to Alex.

"I think you're training is off to a great start, and it is time for a rest," he kindly said, pulling out the chair I was standing next to so I could sit.

I glared at Alex, and he continued to stare at me with a patient smile. Maybe the memories I had about me trying to seduce Alex was all just a dream. He certainly wasn't acting any different.

My father quickly walked over to the stove and put some breakfast in a bowl. He set it down in front of the chair Alex had pulled out, and I sat down. I didn't start eating right away though. I glanced back at Alex, who slid my shirt off the shoulder the Ortal had ripped its claws into. I immediately focused on the table in front of me. He wasn't the slightest bit uncomfortable pulling the shirt off my shoulder. Maybe *more* had happened than I remembered. He didn't say anything, and I hesitantly shifted my eyes to his face.

"How does it feel?" he asked, with a perplexed expression.

"Fine," I answered, not wanting to tell him that it still hurt.

He gently grabbed my wrist and slowly moved it up until I cringed. "Better than I expected."

He lowered it a little, and started to move it backwards. I sucked in the pain, but a small cry escaped my lips.

"I don't need to move my arm back in competition," I hastily said, staring at my breakfast.

"You know that's a lie," Alex stated.

"I can start training again," I argued. If Alex thought I still had a chance, nothing was going to keep me from training.

"How is Alex going to train her?" Krissy interrupted from behind Alex, sounding unusually irritated. "Look at her! She was crazy the last time I saw her! She cut Alex's chest open, and today she can hardly walk."

I felt my stomach drop, but I didn't turn my attention to Alex. I couldn't believe I attacked him. Why was he being so kind to me? He should have left.

"I think," Alex began proudly, "that she is doing extremely well. A person with her injuries wouldn't have attempted walking this morning, let alone come down the stairs."

I could tell by his tone that Krissy's presence annoyed him this morning, and I wondered what she had said to him while I was sleeping.

"Well, it's been what? Six weeks since you brought her back. I want to know what your intentions are."

"Krissy," our father said in warning. "Alex is welcome to our house and everything in it. We should be thankful that he is helping Sonia, especially since you want to marry Kirk."

Krissy opened her mouth as if to argue, but immediately closed it.

"Six weeks…" I thought out loud as the whole world shifted.

The room fell silent, and I felt everyone's eyes on me.

"I'm sorry, Sonia," Krissy said sincerely as she came to my side.

I only remembered two days of the last six weeks. How could I be losing so much time?

"Which makes the Tournament extremely close," my father said for me.

It took everything I had not to cry. I would never be ready. Father put a bowl down for Krissy, and as she sat down, I stood up. I suddenly wasn't hungry, nor did I want to be here. I turned without a word, and walked out of the room. I heard them talking to each other, but I didn't listen. I kept walking until I was outside. I paused for a moment, not paying attention to anything before I started walking up the pathway towards town.

Six weeks? I… I didn't understand how that was possible. Who was Alex kidding? There was no way that I would be ready. It took a lot of effort just to walk. I glanced down at my leg that was aching in protest. Not to mention my shoulder. How was I going to swing a sword? The feeling of hopelessness began to overwhelm me.

I was almost off our land when I heard horses galloping. I didn't pay attention to them until I heard the horses stop a short distance away. Marty was glowering down at me, but I didn't care.

"Up and moving, finally," he smiled, but his tone was not friendly. "I see my brother *is* taking an interest in you," he stated as his eyes looked me over.

I didn't say anything to him. I wanted to drive a sword through him, but I didn't have a weapon, so I tried to will him away. He wanted me out of the Tournament, and now I was.

"I have a new champion," he sneered. "Phillip!"

I watched as a black stallion rode towards us with a man about my age riding on its back. The rider was handsome. He had blonde hair, and the bluest eyes I had ever seen. Phillip had a strong jaw line like Alex, which he showed off... not like Alex who was never clean shaven.

Phillip's gaze abruptly met mine and smiled a warm smile. I immediately tucked my hair behind my ear, looking away.

"This would have been your competition," Marty started.

"Will be your competition," Alex said, stepping next to me.

I watched Marty's eyes grow dark, and a chill moved down my spine. "She will not be ready, *brother*. You shouldn't waste your time. You should..."

"She will be ready, and she will win," Alex assured him.

He clearly hadn't noticed Phillip. Phillip was the epitome of champion.

"She's already wasted too much of my time. Who's going to train her? I don't have the energy for a lost cause."

"I am."

Both Marty and Phillip stared in shock at Alex, but neither said anything.

"Now, if you'll excuse us, we have work to do," Alex said politely.

"You know what you should do, Alex," Marty remarked.

Alex quickly shot Marty an expression of warning that stopped Marty from saying anything more. They glared at each other and I could feel the tension growing between them. I was sure that Marty was going to attack Alex, but neither of them moved.

"Let's go," Marty said with irritation as he glanced at Phillip.

"See you around, Phillip," Alex stated as Phillip rode passed us.

"Uncle," he said with a nod.

What? Hold on a minute.

"That's Marty's *son*?" I said, not even trying to hide my surprise.

Alex laughed. "Yes."

"He looks nothing like him," I commented.

"Phillip looks like his mother," Alex replied.

I stared at Alex as my brain tried to process the information.

"Come, we're going to visit a friend of mine," he said before I could think of anything to say. He whistled loudly, and Storm came galloping up.

CHAPTER SIX

Storm was the biggest horse I had ever seen. I would have to raise my hand above my head to pet his shoulder - if I were allowed to touch him. His body was ripped with muscles and covered with shiny grey fur that was so dark it was almost black.

When I was seven, I had tried to sneak into the stables to get a closer look at Storm, but I ran into my father. He was furious that I wanted to touch the horse, as though Storm wasn't the most magnificent animal we had ever laid eyes on. Alex had entered the stable, but he wasn't nearly as angry. However, with a seriousness I have never forgotten, he told me that I was not to go near Storm.

You would have thought the sheer size of the horse would have kept me away, but it didn't, and that day I saw a challenge. About a week later, I was out in the fields when I spotted Storm grazing. I searched the area until I was confident neither my father nor Alex were nearby. I wandered over towards Storm as though I hadn't seen him until there was only several feet left between us. I was entranced by the power that this horse seemed to emanate, and slowly began to move closer.

Alex appeared out of nowhere, standing between Storm and I. I was angry and was about to fight my way over to Storm, until I glanced up at Alex who wasn't irritated, instead his face expressed his relief. He smiled, telling me he knew that I would attempt to defy him and my father, and he would have been disappointed had I not tried.

He walked me away from Storm, and we sat in the grass on a small hill, admiring the magnificent horse from afar. Alex explained that Storm was a one rider horse who saw all others as a threat, and to attempt to touch Storm when he was not around would have been the death of me. I knew by Alex's tone that he was not exaggerating. I remember glancing at the horse fearfully that day and every day since. I never attempted to go near his horse again.

Storm trotted straight to Alex, and Alex ran his hand down the horse's nose whispering something that sounded foreign. The horse neighed, and pushed him away, causing Alex to laugh. I smiled at the relationship. The amount of fear I had felt as a kid towards that horse was nothing compared to the strength of the relationship between them.

Storm's head came up suddenly as though he just realized that I was there. He walked over to me and I took a few steps back. Storm stared at me before he lowered his head. At first I didn't move. I glanced over at Alex whose face was serious, but relaxed. I didn't know what to do. I wanted to run over to Alex, but I was frozen with fear.

"He is giving you permission to touch him," Alex calmly said.

I focused back on Storm, taking a deep breath to chase away the childhood fear that had surfaced. I slowly lifted my hand, hesitant about touching the mighty steed, but to my surprise the horse gently pushed his head against my palm. I gazed up into his black eye, and a warm feeling washed through me, causing me to smile. Storm softly neighed as I relaxed and nuzzled my right shoulder, causing me to laugh.

"Okay Storm, that's enough," Alex said with humor in his voice. The horse lifted his head and attentively focused him. "We've got things to do."

I watched in amazement as Alex effortlessly leapt onto Storm. He looked magnificent upon Storm, like a warrior from times of old.

"Where are you going?" I curiously asked.

"*We* are going to get you a sword," he casually said.

"I can't afford..." I began, but before I could finish, he snagged me off the ground and placed me in front of him.

"You had better wrap your fingers in his mane," Alex whispered as his left arm secured me to him, and his right hand went into Storm's mane.

I felt like a child, and instantly thought about the time Alex and I had rode into town on my father's horse to go see my first Tournament.

Alex whispered a word I didn't recognize, and Storm began to run. It was exhilarating, and a laugh of pleasure escaped me. I couldn't believe the pace at which we were traveling, we'd be in town in no time.

Storm veered away from town, heading towards the mountains.

"Where are we going?" I asked, not hiding my confusion.

"I told you, to get a sword," he replied.

"But town is the other way," I informed him, knowing he already knew that.

"I am taking you to get a real sword," he said into my ear.

A real sword? What did that mean? The man in town made amazing swords.

✲✲✲

We stopped several hours up the mountain to allow Storm a drink of water. Alex slid off and waited for me to slide down into his arms. He cushioned the drop, and stepped away. I walked over to a tree and sat down, facing the river that Storm had waded into.

"How much further?" I inquired casually.

"We'll be there before nightfall," he replied as he sat down a couple of feet away.

"Before nightfall?" That meant we would not return home today.

"Don't you trust me?" Alex asked.

"You know I do," I replied with a smile, and he smiled back. Memories of the other night entered my mind, making me uncomfortable until I realized that any other man would have taken advantage of my advances.

"Thank you, Alex. For keeping me safe from whatever happened to me. For not…" I quickly

61

focused on my feet. I couldn't finish my thought, and stopped talking.

"I have seen mood swings, but I've never seen a reaction quite like that from the Ortal venom…"

His voice trailed off, and I glimpsed up at him. I could see that whatever he wanted to say wasn't going to be easy for him, and I began to worry about what it could be.

"I…"

"I'm sorry," I interrupted, fearing what he could possibly say.

I stood up, and began walking away from Alex. I did not want to talk about what happened, about my advances on him, or how it made him feel. Whether he was going to say that he cared for me or that he didn't, I didn't want to hear it. The silence between us started to become awkward, and I searched for something to say.

"Thank you for taking me to get a sword," I honestly said over my shoulder.

Storm moved away from the river, and walked towards me. I side stepped and moved around Storm. I walked closer to the river, still thinking about how angry, scared, and sad I had felt. How badly I had desired Alex, and…

Storm neighed softly, pulling me away from my thoughts and I peeked in his direction to see him standing next to me. For a horse that would kill me if I touched it, it sure wanted to be near me.

"Storm is very good at reading people," Alex said. "He doesn't usually like them."

I glanced over at Alex to see him standing near the river's edge. He stepped next to Storm, and put his hand on the horse's shoulder. At his touch, Storm moved his head down to get a drink. I stepped into the river, and waded away from Alex and his horse. I stared down at the over-sized shirt I was wearing, which was all that I was wearing.

"Alex, why are you training me?" I asked as Krissy's words about his intentions entered into my mind.

"I think that people underestimate your abilities."

I stared at Storm, who had moved a little further into the river and closer to me. He stopped only a foot away and I glimpsed at Alex, worried that Storm was going to attack me for riding on him. Not that I had a choice, but did he know that?

Alex smiled, and lifted his chin. I nervously turned my attention back to Storm, who hadn't moved. I took a deep breath, trying to calm my fears. I slowly put my hand up, and cautiously reached towards Storm's head. I ran my hand down the side of Storm's face, and he neighed softly, melting away my fears.

"I haven't seen Storm so intrigued by a person before," Alex quietly said over my shoulder.

I watched his hand follow the same path that mine had, and I turned my head to see that he was staring at Storm with curiosity. I turned to move away from them, but the horse nudged me closer to Alex, and Alex's eyes shifted to my face. Alex stared at me a moment, differently than usual, and I

63

wasn't sure how I felt about that. It wasn't
uncomfortable, just different.

Alex glanced behind me, and shook his head.
"We should get going," he informed Storm.

Storm made a sound similar to an annoyed sigh,
and turned so that we could get on. Again, Alex
jumped effortlessly onto Storm and pulled me up,
wrapping his arm around me. As my hands slid in
the horse's mane, Alex whispered the strange word
and Storm began to run further up the mountain.

We didn't stop again until we had reached our
destination. About a hundred yards or so there was a
large shack, but I couldn't imagine that anyone still
lived there.

"Are you sure your friend is still alive?" I asked.

"Oh, I'm sure," Alex answered as his eyes
scanned the area before he jumped off of Storm's
back. He turned towards me, and waited for me to
slide down, catching me so that the impact of the
ground was soft.

Alex led the way through the woods and Storm
followed several feet back. It was hard to walk
across the rugged terrain because of my leg, but I
wasn't going to say anything. Alex suddenly halted,
and I looked up to see why. He quickly turned,
pulled me close to him, and swung me to the other
side of him as an arrow flew into the tree that I had
been standing in front of.

"Percy!" Alex roared, still holding me securely
to him.

"Alex?" a voice inquired from the shadows.

Storm neighed, sounding annoyed.

"You've... changed. I didn't recognize you."

"We've come to put you to work," Alex loudly said as he let go of me.

"We?" Percy asked in confusion. "Let me see."

Alex took half a step to the side. I glanced up at Alex before I searched the spot that his eyes were focused on. I didn't see anyone.

It was quiet and Alex pulled me closer to his side with one arm, unsheathing his sword from his back with the other. Storm immediately moved to my other side. Everything was creating an unsettling feeling.

"Storm, *you* approve of this... female?" Percy said incredulously. "Isn't she mortal?" he whispered. "Because she smells like it."

Storm blew out air, sounding like he was annoyed.

"Oh right," Percy said as though someone had reminded him of something. "I can't remember the last time you came to visit me, Alex," Percy commented, now standing in front of us.

He was about my height, but only because he was bent over. He wasn't wearing a shirt, and his skinny torso was covered in scars. His long and lanky arms were bent because both his hands were resting atop his bow. His hair was long and white, but I wasn't sure about the color of his eyes.

I found myself wishing I had a sword, but I wasn't sure if it was because of how he looked or if it was because he had referenced me as being a mortal, as though it was unexpected.

65

"Hmm…" Percy slowly moved forward, and breathed the air in deeply. He stared at me for a moment, as though he were thinking things through before is eyes quickly moved to Alex. "What kind of work?"

"She needs a sword," Alex replied, without a touch of request in his voice.

"She? Sword?" I watched Percy ponder these two words.

"Yes," Alex said in a forced kindness.

Percy's eyes shifted away from Alex, and stared at me for a while. He glanced at Storm and then back to Alex.

"A sword," he said as he focused back on me, his eyes searching over me with curiosity.

"A sword," Alex irritably replied.

I glanced up at Alex's face to see him staring angrily at Percy. I was starting to wonder if they really were friends.

"Ortal?" Percy inquired, and I quickly shifted my attention back to Percy who was staring at my shoulder. I glanced down to see that Alex's shirt had slipped off my shoulder.

"Yes," I replied, pulling it back up. My muscles tensed with fear, but I remembered Alex was next to me and forced myself to relax.

"Marty sent her into the Batwas Valley without a weapon," Alex clarified.

"And she survived?"

"Barely," I said.

"What was the reason for that?" Percy asked, talking to no one in particular.

66

"Marty didn't like that I was going to win the Tournament," I replied, focusing my attention on the ground.

"*Thee* Tournament?"

"Yes," I cautiously answered.

"Hates to lose," he said indifferently.

I nodded. I wasn't sure why he had said it, but I did agree.

"He sent *you* alone?" Percy inquired.

"Yes, and without a weapon," I replied hesitantly as I glimpsed at him. I wondered if he always went in circles when he talked with people.

Percy was focused on Alex as though he were trying to solve a puzzle. I glimpsed up at Alex to see that his dark eyes were very focused on Percy. Alex shifted a little, tightening his grip on his sword, and I began to wonder if Alex was going to kill Percy.

"She is…" Percy started, but stopped as Alex shook his head once.

I tilted my head to the side as I stared at Alex. What…

"Well, a sword isn't going to get made standing around out here," Percy irritably said, as though we were the reason he hadn't started yet. He quickly turned, and headed for the shack, disappearing into the woods.

Alex took my hand and led me slowly to the shack, keeping me close to him this time. Storm remained closer to me on the other side, which did not put me at ease. We were halfway to the shack, before the aching in my leg became painful. I

67

clenched my teeth and began to limp, trying to alleviate the pain.

"How's your leg?" Alex softly asked.

"I can manage," I replied, trying to figure out what just happened.

I had no idea if Alex and Percy were actually friends, but I couldn't imagine that they were - Alex still hadn't sheathed his sword. And I did not understand why Percy had looked for clarification from Storm as to whether or not I was mortal. Why had Alex brought me *here*, a little shack in the middle of nowhere, to get a sword?

As we walked into the shack, my jaw hit the floor. "This is amazing," I said in quiet awe.

It wasn't a shack at all on the inside. It was an armory. There were swords of all different lengths hanging on the walls. There were crossbows, axes, and even shields.

"No Percy!!" Alex sternly said and started walking over to him, leaving me to stand in awe by the door. "Don't use that crap. She needs a real sword."

"This is the metal all the men use."

"Which is why we came here. She needs a real sword. Marty is training Phillip, but even if he wasn't, she needs a real weapon. The Alpha tasted her blood."

At the mention of Phillip's name, I shifted my attention to them, and started limping toward Alex. I saw Percy's back straighten at the knowledge that the Alpha had bitten me. To my surprise Percy was a few inches taller than Alex. He seemed quite interested in this new information.

"How do you know that it was the Alpha? Maybe she just fell out of a tree?"

"You only needed one glance to know that it was the Ortal," Alex reminded him.

"It could have been…"

"But it wasn't. It took her six weeks to heal, and she's still struggling."

Percy remained quiet. His hand was rubbing his chin as though he were thinking deeply.

"Phillip?" he said as he dropped his hand. "I didn't think he was old enough to…"

"He's old enough, alright," Alex confidently said.

"They say he's a *charmer*," Percy whispered, as though it were a disgusting fact.

"I'm not worried about that."

"Well you should. Sonia is female," Percy pointed out, and Alex rolled his eyes.

"And a fighter, so let's pull out the good metal."

Percy turned, and almost walked right into me. I noticed that his eyes were green with red cat-like irises, and I tried to hide my surprise. He smiled real big at me and continued on his way.

I made my way over to Alex as quickly as I could, staring at him.

"How are you feeling?" he asked, focusing on my shoulder.

"My shoulder's fine," I told him.

"Do you mind if I check?" he kindly asked.

I shook my head at him. He stepped closer before he slid the shirt off my shoulder, and gently ran his fingers over the healing wounds.

"They look much better," he commented. "Even the color is becoming normal again."

I stared at his face that was close to mine, and his eyes shifted from my shoulder to my eyes. I could see him debating something, but before he could say anything Percy walked back into the room.

"So what weapon does she want, Alex?" Percy said, staring at Alex. Alex quickly took a step away from me, and pulled the shirt back over my shoulder.

"Sonia?" Alex inquired, redirecting Percy's question.

I glanced up at Alex, and he smiled. "I don't understand the question," I hesitantly said.

Percy laughed. "Come here, Sonia."

I limped over to him after I glanced back at Alex, who nodded at me. When I was a few feet from Percy, he motioned to the different sized swords hanging. I was astounded by all the variations. It was overwhelming. I had no idea what I wanted, let alone what would be best for me.

"Which one speaks to you?" Percy asked.

I studied the swords, and then turned my attention to Alex. I hadn't ever had my own sword. I always used someone else's old sword and made it work for me.

"She doesn't know?" Percy said in surprise. "Hmmm… Well, I guess, Alex, *you* will have to tell me what I should do."

"She's left-handed so do not make her a two-handed sword. But, it should not be a short sword," Alex said after looking at me for a few moments.

"Are you sure? Most females…"

"I'm positive, Percy."

"Alright," Percy said, and took some ice-blue metal over to the fire that was burning brightly.

"You should rest. He'll be working at this part for a while," Alex said, but I barely heard him.

The fire had triggered the memories of the two orbs. I could feel my fear and panic as I saw the darkness move behind the Ortal. The events of that night abruptly flooded my senses. Suddenly, I could feel the pain in my shoulder exactly the way I had when the Ortal dug his claws into me and lifted me up, offering me to the orbs of fire in exchange for his life.

I gasped. Was that what it was doing?!

Alex's cool hand moved down the side of my face and rest on my good shoulder, bringing me back to the present. What just happened?

My mind was still panicking, and I anxiously stared at Alex's blurry silhouette. His strong face slowly came into focus. His arm was around me, holding me up because my legs weren't, but that wasn't a concern at the moment. I watched Alex's lips moving and I focused on them, trying to hear what he was saying.

"Sonia," he was calmly calling to me, but he seemed very worried.

"I survived because it was the only way the Alpha would survive," I whispered at the revelation.

71

"Relax," Alex softly said.

I shook my head. The Ortal was…

Alex moved his cheek next to mine and whispered words that I didn't understand, but my body and mind slowly relaxed like he had requested.

CHAPTER SEVEN

"You had better be careful, that's all I'm saying," Percy said in between hits.

"Why do you think I'm here. I…"

"You shouldn't have interfered. The Ortal," Percy interrupted and paused. "You should have left…"

"I couldn't allow them to take her," Alex growled in frustration.

"What are you going to do?" he asked. "Don't you have a similar task? I don't understand how she is still…"

"Jack's family is off limits. That was made clear."

"That was over twenty years ago. Things are changing. And don't tell me you haven't noticed. Marty is slithering his way around the rules as usual. I've heard he is trying to destroy…"

"That is why Sonia needs to be in the Tournament."

"That will only bring more attention to her. Are you sure you've thought this through?"

"The Alpha has already tasted her. She won't be able to hide from them now. She just needs to be in the top two, and I will be able to gain protection for her. Vertas will accept."

73

"The smart thing to do would be…"

"No," Alex growled.

The rhythmic hammering of Percy working began again as silence fell between them. I was instantly awake when the hammering abruptly stopped and Percy let out an irritated sigh. I couldn't believe that the rhythm had almost lulled me back to sleep.

"Alex, what are you doing?" Percy inquired as though Alex's actions were uncharacteristic of him.

"I can't explain it," Alex replied almost inaudibly. The shack was quiet, except for the hammering that began again.

"You really think she can win, especially with Phillip entering?" Percy suddenly asked as he stopped hammering for a moment.

Alex sighed before he spoke again. "He will probably take the win, but she'll be a close second," Alex confidently said. "She is like none I've ever seen. She…"

"Alex?" I called out tiredly, not sure if I was dreaming.

"We were just waiting for you to wake up," he said, sounding unaware that I had heard any of the conversation.

"How long was I asleep?" I asked as he stood over me, worried that he was going to say weeks.

"About twelve hours," he answered and helped me to my feet.

"How's your leg?" he asked.

"Better," I answered. It didn't ache at the moment, and that was a relief.

"This is the fun part," he smiled, stepping away.

He led me over to where Percy was pounding. "I've done everything I could to make sure that Percy made a good weapon, now all you have to do is make it yours."

I started at Alex, not understanding.

"I can't help you," he said. "The rest of this weapon is between you and Percy. Storm and I have to slip out for a few hours, but we'll be back."

I hesitantly nodded, and he smiled with affection. He glanced over at Percy with a serious expression, and I saw the fire reflect in Alex's eyes before he headed towards the door. I watched him walk out the door, telling myself that it was going to be okay. I turned towards Percy to see he was beaming from ear to ear, causing me to feel very nervous.

"So, what am I going to do?" I curiously asked, trying to hide my growing fears. I did not understand how I could help make my sword. I didn't know anything about making a sword.

"We're going to add the design," he said as he showed me the flawless blade that appeared to be muted silver with a hint of the ice blue I had seen earlier.

"All you have to do is sit here," he began to explain as he motioned to a wooden chair that looked very old and uncomfortable. "And let your mind open. Things will begin to shift through your mind, and when you find the one that calls loudest to you, let me know," Percy informed me casually.

75

It sounded easy enough. I walked over to the chair that he had motioned me to sit in. I was surprised to find that it was actually comfortable. I glimpsed back at Percy who was still smiling.

"Close your eyes," he said, and I did as I was told. "Now relax."

That seemed more of a challenging task. I took a deep breath and let it out slowly. Percy began to whisper in his deep voice. I didn't understand the words that he was saying, but they had a rhythm to them that was almost hypnotic and everything relaxed in my mind.

"Now tell me what you see."

There were several images that flowed through my mind. A rose, my mother, the great tree that I had seen as a young girl, Father, Alex, the tattoo that was on his back, and then two orbs of fire began to burn brightly, and all the other images were swallowed by the darkness behind them.

CHAPTER EIGHT

I opened my eyes to the bright sunlight coming in my window. Why did this keep happening? Tears began to slide down my face and onto the mattress beneath me. Anger rushed through me at the thought of ever having seen those orbs of fire. I didn't care if they had destroyed the Ortal. Nothing good had happened since. Every time the orange orbs entered my mind it seemed too much for me, and I would wake up somewhere else.

I closed my eyes as I thought about time passing. I wondered how much time passed this time. Did I actually miss the Tournament?

I angrily sat up, and was taken aback at how well I felt. I uncovered my legs and stared at my left shin. There was nothing there. My heart began to pound. Had it all been a dream? I glanced at my bare shoulder. There was no discoloration or gouges. I quickly stood up, no pain. My heart leapt for joy and I hurried over to Krissy's dresser to look in the mirror. Nothing!

I went over to my dresser and grabbed a pair of pants and a shirt. I dressed in a hurry, but before I reached the door I heard my father yelling outside. I slowly walked over to the window, it sounded like he was in the stable. I couldn't quite hear what he was

77

yelling about, so I climbed out and cautiously walked towards the stable until I heard Father's voice clearly.

"I don't care! You are not allowed to come in here and help yourself to anything…" Father yelled.

I stepped into the barn before the other man replied. "Father, is everything alright?" I asked slowly.

My father focused on me in surprise, but quickly recovered.

"Perhaps you would like to battle my daughter," he growled, and the other man turned around.

"Sonia, I didn't realize this was *your* father," Phillip said.

He remembered me?

I nodded my head and he smiled. His smile made him look perfect, but something inside me was leery of his good looks. Phillip moved closer, and I stepped around him to stand by my father.

"What are you searching for?" I politely asked.

"Alex left something here for my father," he replied.

I doubted that. I wasn't really sure of what I had dreamt and what had really happened at the moment, but Alex would not have left *anything* here for Marty.

"I'm sorry, Phillip, but I don't know what you thought you would find," I said. "Alex doesn't usually leave anything behind."

"That's not what I heard." Again, Phillip smiled and this time he stepped too close to me. "My father assured me that it would be on this property, and I would know it when I saw it."

He was standing a foot away from me, staring at me in a way that made me uncomfortable.

"Perhaps, you should come back later. I'm sure Alex will return shortly," I politely said.

"Really? Father thought he finished his *business* here and left already."

I did not understand what he was getting at. Alex was never here on business. I glanced at my father to see his face turn red with frustration.

I quickly turned back towards Phillip. "Perhaps you should leave now, before we have our first spar," I commented as I stared at him, my irritation rising. "I will not allow my father to become any angrier."

Phillip nodded, "I will tell my father of this information." He smiled at me, and turned to leave. He turned back around before he exited the barn, "I am glad that I came though. Perhaps, I will visit you again."

"I will see you at the Tournament," I replied without a smile.

Phillip continued to smile at me as he nodded. I watched him as he turned and left, hoping he would not come back. After I heard his horse run away, I released the breath that I hadn't realized I had been holding and my father's arms came around me.

"You're okay," he sincerely said.

"What's going on?" I asked, feeling very lost. Something felt terribly wrong, and I was not sure I really wanted to know.

"Alex brought your limp body back a few days ago," he replied, and I stared at him with confusion as panic began working its way into my mind. "He assured me that you were fine, and just needed to rest."

"Back from where?" I hesitantly inquired.

My father's eyes briefly shifted away from me. "I don't know," he lied.

My father rarely lied to me. Why would he now? I stared at him for a few minutes, trying to figure out how to go about finding the answers I wanted. My anger continued to rise as a thought played at the edges of my mind. Did he know why everything bad was happening to me?

I didn't understand why I wasn't just curious, why I felt everyone was against me. I had so many questions swimming around my head that all had to do with...

"What do you know about Alex?" I bluntly asked, trying to calm this ridiculous feeling of distrust.

"What do you want to know?" he countered. He *did* know something?! Percy's words about Alex having a similar task as the Ortal moved into my mind.

"Does he have a family?" I asked, in a forced calm, starting with something simple.

"He considers us his family. And he..."

"Does he have ties to Lord Vertas?" I inquired, thinking of how Alex had saved our land.

"Umm..."

"How does he know so much about healing?"

80

"He's learn..."

"Why does everyone let him do whatever he wants?"

"You don't," he smiled, and I irritably shook my head.

"Where does he go when he leaves here?"

"I don't..."

"What kind of *business* is he doing here?!"

"Phillip, was just..."

"What was Phillip searching for?!"

"Sonia..."

"How is it that you allow Alex..."

"The answers are not his to give," Alex said from behind me. I watched my father relax a little, and I clenched my jaw.

"He is my father," I slowly said as I turned my attention Alex. "He should know about the man whom he allows to take his daughter into the woods, allows to heal her wounds, allows to be alone with her when..."

"You said yourself, I'm kinda like your big brother," he retorted smoothly.

I glared at him, remembering that neither of us was able to make that notion sit comfortably. I turned back towards my father who was now refusing to make eye contact.

"Let's begin your training," Alex said, attempting to change the subject.

"No," I growled, turning towards him. "I don't want your help."

"Sonia," my father said, and I heard his embarrassment, but I didn't care. There were a lot of

81

secrets that stemmed from Alex, and I was beginning to think that being around him wasn't a good idea. If neither of them wanted to tell me what they knew, then I wasn't going to trust either of them.

I wanted to yell at both of them, but I bit my tongue and stormed out of the stable.

"Sonia!" my father yelled after me as if I was five, but I did not pause.

Storm was standing in my way as the setting sun touched my skin. I reached my hand out, and he pushed his nose softly against it. I smiled for a moment, but it quickly faded as I heard someone walking towards me. If Storm wasn't so big, and wasn't Alex's horse, I would have jumped onto his back and rode him out of here, never looking back.

Instead, I took off running for the fields. I could hear my father continuing to call for me, irritation heavy in his voice, but I didn't stop running. I'd deal with his anger when I was ready, until then I would hide in the tall grass and cool off. I sat on the ground and closed my eyes.

Why was I so upset? Alex was only trying to help. Why did I care if he also had another agenda? I wasn't even sure if what I had overheard at Percy's meant anything, let alone if I had really gone there.

Everything seemed so surreal. I couldn't comprehend what was going on. My father seemed to understand what was going on, but he didn't want me to know.

I slid my fingers underneath the neck of my shirt and over my shoulder. I ran my fingers over where I knew the scars from the gouges should be, but there was nothing.

I thought about how there was no pain, no discoloration, and my skin was smooth, as though it never happened. It was like I had dreamt the whole thing. In fact, I probably would have believed that I had imagined the whole thing if Phillip hadn't known who I was.

What did Phillip think that Alex would have left for Marty in the stable? And why hadn't Marty come to get it himself? What did my father know? Why did he *lie* to me? Who was Alex!?

I angrily shook my head. This wasn't helping me calm my mind. I only had three more weeks until the Tournament. That was what my focus should be. I felt my heart sink. I needed a weapon. Marty would never give me the one I had been training with, I was sure of it.

I glanced down at my leg, thinking about how I hadn't been able to walk normal in over six weeks, and now I could run as if, as if… It was so ***impossible***. I closed my eyes, fighting back the tears.

I could remember the pain of the Ortal's teeth ripping through my flesh and crushing the bone. The Alpha had dragged me across the ground that beat up my body, trying to get away from the… shadow.

I could remember the Ortal's strange language and its claws ripping into my shoulder and side. I couldn't escape the memory of the dark shadow that the Alpha feared. The darkness that the Ortal was willing to give me up…

83

The dark shadow *wanted* me? The thought bounced around in my head with a strange amount of confidence.

I breathed in deep at the image of the orbs of fire. The orange orbs that were alive with only energy, I saw no other details in the fire. The darkness that surrounded the orbs was... huge, how could I have not heard any rumors of it before?

The sound of grass moving caught my attention, and I opened my eyes. Dark clouds had rolled in, shortening the twilight. I sat up, and cautiously scanned the area around me. It was probably just the wind that had... I heard the rustling in more than one place this time. No, that was not the wind. I suddenly got the feeling that I was being hunted.

I shook my head. I'm sure I was just being paranoid. I needed to stop thinking about the incident in the valley. I glanced in front of me and fear began racing through me. There were white eyes gleaming in the tall grass. I took a deep breath. This couldn't be happening. I had to be dreaming, I *had* to be!

The gleaming white eyes weren't moving, it should have attacked already. I wondered what it was waiting for. I knew the one in front of me could see me, and knew that I could see it.

I got my feet under me so that I was ready when the Ortal decided to make its move. I heard the language of the Ortal behind me, and I was sure it was speaking to me. I slowly turned around to see the Alpha's face only a foot away from me, its white eyes piercing into me. I could see its pointed teeth as it continued to talk and a chill went down my back, causing alarm to race through my mind. Why had they come here? It licked its lips as it continued to stare at me, and I forced myself to swallow.

I knew I was completely surrounded, that they were faster than me, and I didn't have a weapon, again. I tried to calm my mind, hoping that if I didn't move they wouldn't attack. I watched as the Alpha smiled, and I knew I was in trouble. I quickly turned, jumped over the one I had seen first, and kept running. I heard the Alpha bark, but I didn't look back to see if they were chasing me.

I didn't run towards the house for fear of leading them to Father and Krissy. Instead I ran towards the far end of the field. The Ortal howls filled the night. I didn't know how I was going to survive this time.

My body was pushed to the ground by an invisible force. The next instant, I heard the sound I hadn't heard in six weeks. I quickly rolled over to see nothing and I knew that the large dark shadow was standing between me and the Ortal. As I shifted my attention to the ground, I saw that an Ortal was squashed under its... *foot* that was closest to me.

It's foot! Oh no, no no... It *was* a creature. My mind refused to accept that it was a dragon. No one had...

It roared at them again and the Alpha appeared in an orange glow. The Alpha began to speak as he shamefully lowered his head. I knew that I should run, but I couldn't get my feet to move. The dark shadow made a long warning sounding growl and the Alpha stopped speaking. My heart began to beat

85

faster as the Alpha nodded, and quickly disappeared. Not good.

This time I saw the shadow turn, and as it did I saw two orbs of fire. I couldn't scream, I was too afraid. The two orbs moved closer to me and I saw the energy moving within them, like fire. I wanted to flee, but I couldn't get my legs to move.

I stared into the orange orbs, and became totally captivated. I heard a breath being taken in deeply from the shadow. I slowly moved my shaking hand towards it, expecting my hand to move through it, but instead my fingers touched its smooth... skin? At that moment warm moist air moved across my skin. I stared into the darkness that my hand was touching. I instantly thought of the tattoo on Alex's back. Dragon? The orange orbs were actually eyes? I swallowed hard as I returned my attention to its eyes - my fear slowly abating.

"You're not going to hurt me, are you," I quietly said, feeling confident that it wasn't.

I ran my hand across its snout, towards its eyes. I took a step closer as my hand continued to move along its large head.

It jerked its head up, startling me. What was I thinking?! I should run! I took a step away from it. It immediately focused its attention me and the orbs quickly lowered to the ground. I froze as a soft rumble came from the shadow. Did it know that I was going to run?

I didn't understand what it was doing. Was it hiding? No, that was ridiculous. A creature of this size wouldn't ever hide from anything. Perhaps, it wanted me to hide or... run? Was it going to kill me when I did?

The orbs of fire moved towards me, and I began to step away. The orbs moved quickly to prevent me from moving away, and began moving toward me again. I began to move backwards and the orbs slowly continued to move closer until I backed into something. I glanced over my shoulder to see the darkness. The shadow nudged me towards the solid darkness behind me, and I glimpsed back at the orbs, but they were gone. Again the darkness touched me.

What did it want with me? I tried to side step, but the orbs appeared again. I put my hand behind me, feeling the shadow behind me and realized that if I lifted my leg high enough I could move over the darkness. I didn't like that idea, and tried to move passed the orbs again. They disappeared and the darkness lightly pushed me back. I shook my head, this was insane! Again the orbs of light appeared and moved towards me. I quickly decided that stepping over the darkness was my only chance. However, as soon as one leg was over the darkness, it moved and I closed my eyes, clinging to its... neck, holding on for my life.

The darkness was smooth, had a neck, could touch me, and breathe. The orbs of fire had to be eyes, but this could not be a dragon. I didn't want to die.

The wind whipped around me and as moisture covered my skin, I opened my eyes. I couldn't see anything, but blackness. Suddenly there was bright light blinding me. As my eyes adjusted, I clung tighter to the darkness, but I couldn't close my eyes. I was so amazed at the sight before me, how white the top of the dark clouds were. I had never thought about the possibility before.

As I started to focus on the sky around me, I saw the outstretched darkness that looked like a wing. I quickly shifted my attention to the other side... wings? My mind froze at the conclusion that I refused to believe. Dragons hadn't been seen in... forever.

I lifted my face up, staring at the long neck that did not reflect the light from the sun, at all. Its neck *looked* like it was covered in scales and yet it was soft to my touch. I released my hold with one arm, and ran my fingers down the side. Its skin was smooth and soft, like a baby's skin, but I could see each individual black scale that covered it.

The darkness suddenly started to dive, and again I clung to its neck. I had just upset it! I was going to die! Of course I was. It was a dragon!

CHAPTER NINE

I felt the cold wet moisture as we went back *through* the cloud. We landed in a field in the middle of a forest, and relief washed through me that I was still alive.

It was only a moment before panic began to race through me again as I realized I had no idea where it had taken me. I briefly glimpsed over at its head and then back down at its neck. The Ortal had cowered before this creature, but that didn't make it my friend.

It slowly lowered its entire body close to the ground, and after quick debate, I decided to get off. If it was going to kill me, there was nothing I could do about it.

I slid down, and stepped several feet away from it. It stayed laying on the ground as I stared at its strong lean body. It had folded its black wings against its body. Had I not watched it do it, I would have thought that the wings had disappeared. It had a long thick tail that tapered off behind it.

As my eyes followed its massive body - that stood more than twice as tall as me - back towards its head, I met its eyes that looked like balls of fire in the night sky. The orbs of fire slowly moved closer to me. Its eyes were hypnotic, even with the fear that was racing through me I didn't shift my eyes away, and I didn't run. There were different shades of the brilliant orange that seemed to be dancing in its eyes.

As I continued to gaze at them, a sense of familiarity moved over me, causing my mind to relax. Slowly, the details of its dark face began to become clearer to me. I moved my eyes along its triangular shaped snout and down to its partially opened mouth. I could see the tips of its sharp silver teeth and my breath caught. The creature closed its mouth, as if realizing the fear that had arose in me.

I cautiously took a step closer and slowly lifted my trembling hand, knowing that it was watching me intently. I touched its smooth face, and it breathed in. I quickly glimpsed at its eyes to see that the orbs of fire had disappeared. Was it annoyed with my touch or did it like it?

Rain began to drip on my skin before I realized the storm had moved over us. In an instant I was soaking wet, but the storm was insignificant at the moment. I heard the thunder as the creature opened its eyes becoming the shadow from my memories again, but this time it didn't frighten me.

I turned away from the orbs of fire, and slowly began to walk toward its wing. I did not stop touching the creature, for fear of losing sight of it. It allowed my hand to slide across its face and along its long neck.

I stopped and stared at its dark body. I was fascinated with how the water repelled off its skin. I glanced over my shoulder to look at its face, but I could not see the orange eyes.

I was shivering from the cold air that was whipping the rain around me. I wrapped my arm that was not touching the dragon tightly around myself. I should have started to search for shelter, but I did not want to move away from this creature. I glanced back into the darkness that I could feel, and continued to walk towards its wing. As my fingertips skimmed across its powerful body, I could feel its thick muscles begin to relax at my touch.

I was certain that this was a dragon, but I couldn't believe it. A creature from the Ancient's realm, a creature that no one had seen in... who knows how many generations, a creature that the stories told only brought death, was here, allowing my touch. The rain stopped abruptly, but I could still hear it falling, and the rumbles of thunder continued to move through the sky. I stared up into the dark storm to see nothing but darkness, not even the lightening that should be flashing brightly all around.

Had the dragon put its wing over my head? It was the most logical explanation.

"Thank you," I softly said through chattering teeth.

I felt a rush of warm, moist air gust passed me, and terror flooded into my mind, but as I turned to see the orbs of fire, all I saw was blackness. I leaned my back against its large, surprisingly warm body, and lowered myself to the ground. The heat of its body instantly began to warm me.

The storm raged on, but I could not feel any of it anymore. It's protecting me from the storm? It protected me from the Ortal twice now. I shook my

91

head at this creature's actions. Dragons did not protect people, ever. And yet, here I was, being protected.

"Why me?" I whispered.

Of course there was no answer, and more questions began growing in the silence. I rested the side of my face on my arms that were folded around my knees. I stared towards the front of the dragon, seeing only darkness. I listened to the sounds of the relentless storm, feeling surprisingly safe. All of my fear and panic had disappeared.

I thought about Alex's tattoo. Did he know about this dragon? Did he...

Cool air brushed across my body, and the rain began dripping on my skin. I glanced up in surprise to see that the storm had passed, leaving me in its wake with a creature that wasn't supposed to exist, that wanted to keep me safe, and still no explanation for anything that was happening to me.

The moonlight began to filter through the clouds before I stood up. I slowly turned around and stepped back, taking in its size with each step I took. I watched as it stood, doubling its height. I suddenly felt very insignificant, even with the knowledge that it was protecting me. The world suddenly felt so big, and I couldn't wrap my head around the truths that I now could see. I was shivering again, but it really didn't matter to me that I was cold and wet as I stared at the shadow in front of me.

The orbs of fire appeared, and I knew that it was very interested in me. I watched it step closer, lowering its head. I put my hand out and stared into its eyes. As its nose touched my hand, my fingers slowly slid along the side of its snout. It breathed in deeply at my touch, and a strange sensation moved through me, but it did not alarm me. Instead, I found that it only increased my desire to be near it. In fact, I was finding that I didn't want to go home at all.

To my disappointment it began to nudge me over to its neck again. I slowly moved in the direction that it was gently pushing me, but I didn't step over its neck right away. Instead, I turned to gaze upon its captivating eyes.

"Why are you protecting me?" I asked quietly, watching the shades of orange move in its eyes. I continued to watch the fire in its eyes, and after a moment it nudged me again. I put my hand on its snout, wondering why I was so comfortable being so close to it now.

I slid my hand across its neck before moving one leg over it. It stood up slowly, taking off as if there were no gravity. I held tightly to it, not because I was worried about falling, but because I wanted to be close to it. The sense of security that I felt was incredible, and I closed my eyes for a moment as I breathed in deeply at the tranquility that flowed through me.

I watched the clouds thicken again as it flew. The moonlight reflecting off the white clouds was magnificent, and I was amazed at the beauty of it, but not nearly as captivated as I was by the creature I was riding. I wasn't ready for us to head back to the ground, I wanted to stay up here. However, it dived into the white clouds, only to land in the darkness and rain. It lowered itself to the ground and I slid off.

I quickly turned and ran my hand along its smooth, soft skin. The Shadow Dragon, the most amazing creature I had ever seen.

I very slowly backed away a couple of steps, but I remained focused on the darkness that I knew was the Shadow. The cold rain was falling hard, and the wind was relentless, but I had no intention of walking any further away from it. The Shadow nudged me to turn around.

As I did, I saw the lights of a house about a hundred feet away. I shook my head as it pushed against my back, moving me towards the lights.

"Please," I began, but a gust of wind pushed against me, and I knew that it had left. I stood in the rain, staring into the night, feeling so very lost.

My shivering body brought me back to reality. I wrapped my arms around myself, and shook my head against the confusion I felt inside before I began to run toward the lights. Just before I reached the door, I ran into something and fell to the ground. I glanced up to see Alex soaking wet too.

"There you are," he said with relief. "Jack," he called loudly over his shoulder as he crouched down and scooped up my body that was shivering uncontrollably. He held me tightly to his chest, and the warmth of his body began to warm mine.

"Sonia!" my father exclaimed shortly after the door opened. "I was so worried that the Ortal had taken you. Alex has been searching for you..." I heard the parental frustration in his voice, but just listened to him as he began to yell because he had been truly worried about me. "I'm so glad that you found her," my father said as he glimpsed up at Alex. "Set her down on the couch. Where did you find her?"

"Just outside the door. She ran into me," he began to explain as he set me on the couch, and moved away so my father could move closer to me.

"What were you thinking?!" Father continued to scold me. "You know what's out there!"

I couldn't help but glance over at Alex. I felt awful that he had been searching for me in this weather. His clothes were soaking wet and his hair was dripping water into his face. To my surprise there was a subtle smile on his face, and I smiled back.

"This is serious you two!" my father growled, as though we were a couple of kids.

"Jack, she's alive," Alex said calmly with a touch of humor in his voice as he ran his fingers through his black hair, preventing the water from streaming down his face.

"Out of sheer luck!" my father retorted.

"Maybe," he conceded, but his voice portrayed that he thought it was more than just luck.

My father locked eyes with Alex, and I wasn't sure I understood the expression he gave Alex, but Father calmed down. "You look like you're fine, Sonia. Why don't you go change," father told me, "you're shivering."

I nodded to him and stood up. I walked towards my room, glimpsing up at Alex as I passed him. He smiled affectionately, and I quickly focused on my door. I hurried into my room, shutting the door behind me. I quickly went to the window and searched the sky. The rain had slowed, the lightning was in the distance, and the thunder rolled faintly.

"What are you looking for?" Krissy suspiciously asked as she turned the light on.

I quickly turned in shock. I hadn't expected her to be in here.

"I was just watching the storm," I replied.

I watched her walk over to me, and I knew she was annoyed by something.

"The storm, huh," she said as she joined me by the window, her eyes not on the sky. There was a touch of bitterness in her voice that surprised me.

"Yes," I replied, slightly annoyed.

"I'm glad that you are… safe."

"Are you?"

"I am. I just find it very interesting that Alex has taken an awful lot of…*interest* in you," she commented as though Alex and I never spent time together when he was visiting.

That threw me for a loop, and I stared at her curiously. Alex and I always hung out together.

"Father makes time for you two to be alone every chance he gets, whereas he used to get frustrated with Alex and you. Don't think I haven't noticed. Alex takes you away for a few days, and dad acts like you left with your girlfriend… if you had one." She smiled insincerely at me before she continued. "And then Alex is out searching for you long after everyone else has stopped, including

Father. And look at you, you're not the least bit frazzled."

"You're mad because Alex was out trying to find me?"

"Come on, Sonia. You expect me to believe that you weren't with him all this time? I mean how convenient that you return at the same time…"

"What are you saying Krissy?" I asked with irritation.

"I thought you said that boys weren't of any interest to you."

"I don't have time for them," I replied defensively.

"Alex is a…"

"Alex is father's friend!" I angrily said. How dare she imply such a thing. "And even if he wasn't, he is too much of a gentleman. Not to mention way out of my league. I'm an ordinary girl who knows no one. I'm a nobody. He is far from ordinary, and knows people like Lord Vertas!" I paused for a moment and glared at her. "If you're jealous, then that's your problem, you shouldn't have passed on him for a man that was afraid of his own shadow."

"What!? Kirk…"

"Kirk is a wimp compared to Alex. Kirk kisses you as soon as he gets you alone. Forces you to think you have to stay with him because you're worried about what other people will think."

"Alex has nothing on Kirk," she growled furiously. "Kirk *is* a gentleman, and thinks that there is more to this life than how to handle a sword."

97

I laughed. "I can totally see why you're frustrated. Kirk isn't half the man you could have had. Alex has seen the world, you can have an intelligent conversation with him, he sees the world like no one else, and he isn't afraid of anything! He is honest and compassionate…"

"There *is* something going on between you two. Look how you're defending him."

"No. I respect Alex. He's done so much for this family."

"I don't trust Alex. Kirk says…"

"What has Kirk done for this family? I mean he's waiting for *me* to win the Tournament so you two can get married. It's because of Alex that we're even here!"

I watched her face become vehement. I suddenly felt very sad, I shouldn't have said that.

"At least we haven't had sex," she hissed.

I turned and stormed over to her. I watched the fear enter her eyes.

"We both know that's not the truth. You can lie to everyone all you want, but I know the truth," I snarled quietly. "Alex is my trainer, and he is father's friend. The only thing Alex has done for me is keep me from dying. If you even *try* to taint his reputation, I will make your life even worse. I know your secrets. I don't need rumors or theories."

With that I turned and walked out of the room. I glanced up to see both my father and Alex staring at me in shock, neither of them saying a word.

"Alex, I think I am ready for you to begin training me," I stated as I headed for the door, anger still strong in my voice.

Alex turned and followed me out, closing the door behind him. I walked through the puddles and muddy ground. I entered the stable before Alex said anything.

"It's late and you're cold," Alex said as though he were reminding me.

"I don't care!" I snarled at him.

"We should go back in the house, so you can change and get a good night's sleep."

"I can't sleep," I growled. "And if I go near Krissy, she won't live to see tomorrow."

He smiled at me and stepped closer. "You haven't trained in…"

"All the more reason we should start now!" I interrupted, trying to control my anger. I wasn't mad at him.

"In the morning," he said sternly, and I glared at him. I was not a child.

"*You* go and get some rest, *I'm* going to practice," I said in a forced calm.

I watched his face become irritated. "I haven't had to do this in a long time," he informed me, and moved so quickly that I didn't have time to dodge him. He picked me up, and threw me over his shoulder. "You have been through enough for one day."

"Put me down!" I snarled at him.

He was done talking to me, and I began hitting my fists against his back. He carried me in the

99

house, as though I wasn't struggling to get free. He really hadn't done this in a long time. I think I was thirteen the last time this had happened.

I knew at this point that my struggle was just wasted energy, but I had hoped that, being older, I could swing my weight and get away, but I couldn't. I stopped struggling, and decided I would just climb out of the window after he put me in my bed and left. However, he did not take me to my room. He was headed up the stairs.

"Everything okay?" my father called after us.

Alex didn't say anything to my father. He didn't say anything until he dropped me on his bed. I sat up, and was contemplating making a break for the door.

"You won't make it," he informed me. "You think I don't know you better than that," he said.

I scowled at him, thinking maybe I would try to prove him wrong, even though I knew he was right. He would have me in his arms before my feet ever hit the ground.

I continued to glare at him while he just stared at me with his kind eyes.

"Now, you might as well lay down and get some sleep."

I flopped down onto my side with my back to him. I felt a blanket fall across my body, warming me instantly - I had forgotten I was cold. The warmth of the blanket felt good, and slowly my anger drained out of me.

"Thank you, for the blanket," I whispered.

The bed shifted a little as he had laid on the bed. I didn't have to look to know that he was staring up at the ceiling. This was how we always ended up. Him laying a short distance away from me, waiting for me to calm down so he could explain the error of my ways or describe a solution to my problem.

"Thank you," he softly said.

"For what?" I asked as I rolled over so I could see him.

"Rest," he whispered as he gazing at me. "We'll start training tomorrow."

I didn't want to close my eyes. I was suddenly worried that he was going to be gone in the morning.

"I will train you," he assured me. "Rest."

My eyes closed against my will and I relaxed, knowing he wasn't going to leave tomorrow.

CHAPTER TEN

When my eyes finally opened it was mid-morning, and Alex was gone. I knew that he had waited for me to fall asleep before he went down to the couch, just to make sure I didn't try to leave. I had been able to sneak out once when I was a kid, but never again. I smiled at the memories of how patient he had always been with me. It was surprising really. I hadn't known anyone with the compassion and patience Alex had shown me.

I sat up, and saw the folded clothes on a chair. I pulled off the clothes that were still damp, and put the clean ones on. After I was dressed, I left the room and ran down the stairs. I hadn't expected Alex to still be on the couch.

He turned his attention to me, "Sleep well?"

"You know I did," I said, pretending to still be annoyed with him.

He smiled, knowing that I wasn't the least bit annoyed with him. "Why don't you go get some food," he suggested. "Then we'll start."

I smiled back, and nodded. I walked into the kitchen to find Krissy sitting on Kirk's lap. They both looked up at me in surprise. I turned away from them and walked to the counter, grabbing a bowl and spoon before dishing some breakfast out of a pot on the stove. Now I knew why Alex was still in the living room.

I heard Krissy giggling, but I ignored it. I didn't care what they were doing or saying - I didn't care about them at all. The kitchen door opened and closed and I was relieved that they had left.

"Have a good night sleep?" Kirk inquired.

Great. She left *him* in here with me. I thought I made it clear that I disliked him. I guess she wanted to continue to annoy me.

"There are a lot of rumors going around town about Alex, Marty, and you," he commented.

So what. I started eating my breakfast with my back to him, hoping he would take a hint.

"They say that you were only on the team because Marty fancied you."

A small burst of laughter escaped my lips. Yea, that's a good one.

"They say, Marty sent you to the Batwas Valley because he was bored with you. You were unable to *satisfy* him."

I rolled my eyes, and continued eating my breakfast.

"If you like older men..." he whispered in a suggestive tone that I did not like.

The chair slid away from the table, and I heard him walking toward me. I turned, and glared warningly at him.

"Got to love what **They** say," I smiled insincerely. "The reason Marty sent me to the Batwas Valley," I continued in a serious tone, "is because I am a better warrior than all of *they,* and *they* all know it. But how would that look if *they* had to tell everyone that?"

"Are you going to try and convince me that a little girl like you could beat the best men in this land?"

"I'm not going to *try* anything," I answered. I was irritated that Krissy sent Kirk to finish our argument.

"You know, Krissy wishes Alex had taken your father up on his offer all those years ago."

"I don't blame her, because then she wouldn't have settled for a fake like you," I remarked.

His hand came up and he attempted to strike me, but I blocked with my forearm and hit him in the gut.

"Why you little…"

"Sorry, Kirk, but I find nothing intimidating or interesting about you. I mean, waiting for me to win the Tournament to marry my sister? How cheap are you really? If you actually loved her you would have already married her. So, don't think for one minute that I think you're worth looking at."

I watched his face redden with anger.

"Oh, because Alex is a great catch," he haughtily replied. "He couldn't find a woman his age, so he preys on a girl years younger than himself."

"You know nothing about Alex," I calmly said.

"What do you know about him?"

"He's done more for this family than we deserve. He works hard without asking for anything in return. He…"

"Why?" he asked like a snake. "Why would he try to get in good with your father? Spend all his time with a young girl, if he weren't after something?"

"Not every guy is like you, thankfully."

"I think that if you've already been had, then why not me too."

"You're marrying my sister," I said, suddenly very confused.

"She doesn't want me, she wants Alex. It's always been Alex," he bitterly stated. I could tell by his face that he wasn't lying. He was furious that Krissy was indeed settling for him. "I told her if she wanted him, then she should go get him... and I will prevent you from interrupting."

I balled my fist up. "Take one more step, and you'll wish you hadn't," I growled as memories flashed through my mind. She had always been trying to get his attention? All this time she had been trying to make him jealous?

"Maybe his sudden interest in you, is to make Krissy angry for getting engaged."

I shook my head. "Alex isn't *interested* in me."

"But he's putting on a good show."

"I don't know what you're talking about..." I said and kicked at him as he lunged for me.

He ran at me again, and I slammed my fist into his face. I quickly turned with a kick, knocked him into the counter, and watched as he sunk to the floor. I quickly walked out of the kitchen to get away from him before he got back up. As I stepped into the room, I saw my sister hanging onto Alex's shoulders, holding her body against his.

Whatever, I thought and walked passed them without a glimpse at Alex. I continued outside, Alex could catch up when he was done. There was a reason that I didn't find boys interesting, and this was just the tip of the iceberg. I started walking toward the fields, breathing in the morning air.

Of all the things that just happened, Kirk's advancement on me was the only thing I was surprised at. Why he thought I would allow him to touch me was a whole different story. I couldn't believe what Kirk had said. My sister did not like Alex. She would have mentioned it at some point. I shook my head at the image of her hanging on Alex.

"I think now would be a good time to practice with your sword," Alex suggested from behind me.

I turned toward the stables and away from him. I would grab a horse, and go for a ride. This morning was all wrong, and I wanted out of here.

"Sonia…"

"I don't have a sword," I reminded him without hiding my irritation, wanting him to go away.

"Sonia, I'm here to train you. I told you that last night."

I turned to see that Storm was standing next to him. Was he going to leave now? Of course he was going to leave. I continued to head to the stables. I really didn't want him to leave, but I knew that I would never be able to change his mind.

"Sonia, what is wrong?" he asked as I entered the stable.

What was wrong?! I searched through my frustration, trying to recall a question that I needed an answer to.

"Why? Why are you training me?" I asked as the feelings of being lost resurfaced.

"Have you changed your mind about being in the Tournament?" he asked curiously. I shook my head, and the clarity of what was important focused my mind. "I could leave, if that is what you want."

"How could you ask that?" I inquired. His eyes searched my face for a moment before he smiled.

"I think that we should stay by the house, since there were signs of Ortal in the fields."

"Alex, how are you going to train me when I do not have a... sword?"

My voice trailed off as I watched him pull out two sheathed swords from the pack on Storm. After he strapped his sword to his back, he moved closer to me.

"This is your sword," he informed me, handing the other sheathed sword to me. "I have to admit, Percy did a spectacular job."

He held the sheath so that I could pull the sword out, but I didn't right away. I couldn't believe that I had my *own* sword. I just stared at the handle. It was amazing. The handle was wrapped in peculiar black leather. The hilt held a square, sparkling pink-rose colored gem that was about an inch in diameter.

I slowly wrapped my fingers around the handle, and slid the blade out of its sheath.

The blade was about two inches wide, and the metal was polished to a brilliant shine. There was an ice-blue tint to the metal, making it appear that much more exquisite. The blade was sharpened on both sides and came to a point. On the blade was the *Shadow*. I swallowed hard as I stared at the image. Somehow Percy was able to craft gems into the metal that made the eyes gleam orange.

I quickly shifted my eyes to Alex, who was watching me intently.

"Do you know about this creature?" I curiously asked.

He smiled. "It's a dragon."

"Why did Percy put a dragon on my sword?" I asked, trying to sound casual.

It wasn't that there was a dragon on the sword that had me feeling anxious, but that it was the *Shadow* he had crafted perfectly onto the blade. At the time the sword was made I didn't even know the shadow was a dragon. How...

"He said that it was the strongest image that you showed him."

How did Percy know that?! I don't remember saying anything. I immediately focused on Alex, expecting him to begin questioning me, but he didn't.

"But they don't..." I started, but I couldn't finish my thought.

"I think we both know that they do," he whispered.

"You've seen a dragon?" I inquired with amazement.

"I know they exist," he answered with a gentle smile.

I quickly looked down at my blade again. "What are these symbols for?"

"They are symbols of an ancient language."

"Do you know what they mean?"

This time he only nodded.

"You're not going to tell me are you?"

"Let's practice," he answered, and pulled his sword out.

His blade was very elegant. From the first moment I saw it, it had always intrigued me. There were symbols on his blade that were similar to the ones on mine, except they moved along his blade, creating what looked like a flame.

I watched Alex slowly raise his sword into a high guard, and I took a low protective stance.

"It's been a while, so let's walk through it. Okay?"

I nodded, and waited for his attack. It came very slowly, giving me lots of time to block. I pushed his blade away, and then attacked. We went back and forth in this overly slow form for an hour or so before we gradually moved the blades faster.

"You're dead," he said, holding his blade at my neck. I growled at him, and he smiled. "Let's take this outside."

As soon as I stepped out of the stable he moved in on the attack, and I brought my sword up. He sped the pace up even more, and we moved all over the open area around the house. Nothing in the world existed except my desire to win.

"Dead," he smiled and we continued.

109

"Dead," he said several minutes later and quickly moved away, but attacked again just as fast.

Again and again, he moved fluidly and swiftly. He was so much better with a sword than I was, but that didn't lessen my desire to win.

"Dead."

"Ahh!" I yelled irritably. He wasn't even trying his hardest. I wanted to win, and began to move faster. My growing frustration caused the battle to gain intensity and last longer, but ended with me on my back.

"Dead."

When he removed his sword from my neck, I was on my feet and attacking. To my amazement I knocked the sword from his hand. Unfortunately, he grabbed my wrist and twisted until my hand let go of my sword. I brought my foot up and attempted to knock him away but I was unable to budge him.

I glanced up at Alex to see he was smiling.

"Yes, I know... *dead*," I said with frustration.

"You need to watch this side when you're fighting, and remember to not ground yourself. I know that I..."

"Taught me better," I irritably finished for him as the feeling that he was disappointed swept through me.

His face softened after a moment. "Thank you for defending me so boldly," he said, not moving away.

"Krissy and Kirk have no right to threaten your reputation," I replied, and the anger at them resurfaced.

110

"I don't think it was *my* reputation that they were lashing at," he quietly said.

The idea that Krissy was attacking *my* virtue hadn't even crossed my mind. "I don't think it would matter what she said about me… everyone would probably cheer if what she was saying was true. I mean look how Kirk reacted."

Nothing Krissy could say about me affected me, I didn't care what anyone thought. Alex loosened his hold on me and I moved away. I bent down to pick up my sword. As I wrapped my fingers around the handle, the orange eyes on my sword caught the sunlight and gleamed brightly.

"Alex?" I asked as stood, not certain if I should ask the question that floated in my mind.

"Yes?" he replied.

I turned to face him, hesitantly looking at his face. "Why would a dragon decide to protect a…"

"Lady."

I smiled at the compliment and nodded. He walked over to the hill we were standing near, and sat down. I walked over and sat down next to him. I wasn't irritated that he decided that we were going to take a break, because as usual, he seemed to know that I needed one.

"There are many legends to pick from. It's been so long since a dragon has shown itself in these lands."

"Did you see it?"

"I believe that you did, especially since it is detailed so perfectly on your sword."

"Percy could have…"

111

"No, he only draws what you show him. It makes the sword stronger for you."

That created more questions, but I didn't want to move away from the dragon, so I didn't ask any of the new questions that surfaced.

"What are the legends you know of?" I asked. "All I've ever heard are stories of their cruelty."

Alex ran his hand through his hair before his eyes focused on me.

"It is said that sometimes a dragon shows itself because a strong spirit has been found. Sometimes a dragon shows itself because the Dark Forces are attempting to take over this world. The romantic legends say that a dragon can fall in love…"

"With a person?" I interrupted incredulously.

He nodded. "A bond is formed that is beyond their control."

"How would that work?" I inquired, thinking about the size of the Shadow Dragon.

I shook my head, that theory seemed outrageous. I had always thought the romantics were crazy.

I glanced over at Alex to see that he had laid back, and was now staring up at the stars that had appeared in the wake of the sunset. We had practiced all day? How had I not noticed? I guess it didn't really matter, since there was nothing else I'd have rather been doing.

I laid back next to him and gazed into the sky. I thought about how the world had suddenly become so big and new.

"You are naturally gifted with the sword," Alex said after a few minutes, breaking the silence.

"Yea," I said sarcastically. "I only died how many times?"

He laughed, "Luckily, you're not going up against me."

I laughed too. It had been a long time since we had done this. After my mother disappeared this was where I had always come to get away from the world. When Alex came, he was the only one who knew where I would be. He always found me out here. Instead of being irritated or angry, like my father used to get, Alex would lay next to me and we would gaze into the sky together. He would tell me stories, or jokes, or theories he had heard about - depending on what my needs were.

It took me a long time to get over my mother's disappearance. It was Alex that had helped me begin to accept it. Her disappearance was the reason I fought so hard. I didn't ever want to *disappear*. I refused to believe that just because I was a girl, I couldn't help protect my family or myself.

I had seen Alex practicing with his sword one day, and my father caught me, which wasn't bad until I told him I wanted to learn. At which point he gave me more chores, and told me that a girl did not learn the sword or any fighting for that matter.

I, of course, didn't agree. I used to hide in a tree for hours, and watch Alex practice. Then, when all my chores were done, I'd take a stick and imitate what I had seen. My father had been furious when he discovered me practicing, but Alex stepped in. He told my father that it would strengthen me and help me fight against my loss, helping me to open up

113

again. Things in my life always seemed better when Alex was around.

"Thank you for coming back," I said as I thought about how he was once again helping me overcome more obstacles. "I'm sorry for being so angry with you earlier. I feel awful that you were searching for me in the storm."

"Don't apologize."

I looked away from the stars and over at him. He was not gazing into the sky either, he was staring at me.

"I'm sorry that your world is changing so abruptly," he softly said.

"Is that why you stay?" I asked.

"Yes."

I wanted him to explain, but I knew he wouldn't because he turned his attention back to the sky. I stared at him a moment longer before I gazed back up at the stars. I was surprised at how relaxed I felt laying here in the dark, especially after all that had happened. I breathed in deep, trying to allow myself to be content with the way things were.

"Do you think that the *Dark Forces* are rising? Is that why the dragon has come?" I asked, no longer able to fight the questions that were running through my mind.

"I think that only the dragon knows the answer to that."

I didn't say anything more, even though I wanted to ask a million more questions. I knew that he would dodge all my inquiries, and leave me with more questions... although I wasn't sure that was possible.

"We should probably head back," he said quietly. "I don't want to give your sister more ammunition."

I turned my head to see that he was smiling humorously and I smiled. He stood up, helped me to my feet, and we walked back towards the house. Alex picked up his sword as we passed it, sheathing it behind him. I sheathed my sword, but continued to hold it in my hand. I kept my eyes to the sky, hoping to see the Shadow... dragon.

Alex opened the door and held it open for me. I glanced at him and then stepped in to hear Krissy stop mid-sentence. She glared at me, and I turned toward Alex.

"Thank you, Alex," I said to him and he smiled with affection, causing me to smile bigger because I knew he was just upsetting Krissy on purpose.

"Good night, Father," I said, looking at him before I turned toward my room without a glance at Krissy.

I walked to my bed, and slid my sword under my pillow. I laid on my bed, and immediately rolled onto my side so that I could see out the window.

I thought about the dragon and the reasons that Alex said it might have shown itself. I highly doubted that it was in love with me since we had just met, not to mention how highly improbable that was. There were Dark Forces in the world, but I didn't understand what it meant if they were on the rise. However, that was something I could believe. Father

115

and Alex both have said I have a strong spirit… not always in a positive manner, but they have said it just the same. However, a person saying that one had a strong spirit was not the same as a dragon seeing it, I was sure.

I shook my head, knowing that I would probably never understand. I continued to stare out the window, wondering if I'd ever understand my part in it until my eyes no longer stayed opened.

CHAPTER ELEVEN

The sun woke me, and I immediately sat up. I quickly changed my clothes, grabbed my sword, strung it across my back and ran out of the house. To my amazement, Alex was not waiting for me and I smiled. It had been two weeks, and I hadn't been able to beat Alex outside yet. I ran towards the woods that I knew well. I sprinted through the trees hurdling the fallen trees, ducking under the low branches, feeling the adrenaline push the excitement through me until I was deep in the woods.

I closed my eyes for a moment before I unsheathed my sword. Once I was focused, I opened my eyes and pretended that I was surrounded by the enemy. I slashed at the invisible foes and dodged *their* weapons. I continued to move through the woods swinging my sword and eluding my imagination.

I felt myself tiring, but I continued to push through it. The Tournament was going to start in three days, and I had to be ready. I was back to my normal abilities amazingly enough, but I knew Phillip was expected to win and *I* wanted to win.

Alex had been teaching me every day from sun up until I could barely stand or lift my sword. He had started by taking it easy on me, but still

117

challenging me. However, each day he challenged my abilities a little more, and I would always push harder. I loved these days filled with training. Alex kept me from all distractions by bringing me into the woods a mile or so away from my father's land. From the moment I woke up until the minute I fell into bed there was only me and my ambition to be the best swordsman in the land.

I only saw Krissy when we returned, and I was too exhausted to care about anything she had to say or whatever actions she was taking to sway my focus. After the first week she stopped completely, and the last few days I hadn't even seen her.

Even the orbs of fire had stayed out of my consciousness. Part of me wondered if by knowing that the orbs were actually the eyes of a dragon had made it all sit better with me. It was beyond my understanding why a dragon was protecting me, and Alex kept me so busy that I had little time to think any more about it.

Reality tried to seep into my pretend world, and I focused harder on my imagined opponents. I stabbed and then turned with my sword leading and heard it clang against metal, forcing me out of my imaginary battle. I glimpsed up to see Alex standing in front of me.

"You still have an amazing imagination," he smiled, "but I think you need to battle a person," he commented.

I smiled at him, wondering how long he had been watching me. I pushed his sword away from mine and watched a devious smile cross his lips. I quickly started my attack on him.

He stayed on the defense for the most part and I knew he wasn't trying, but I didn't mind too much because I was tired.

"Is that all you've got?" he laughed after we had moved even deeper into the woods. "Perhaps, I have picked the wrong…"

I scowled at him and began to swing harder, focusing my hits because I knew he was right, I had gotten lazy. My opponents weren't going to care if I was tired. I needed to pull my energy up and fight harder.

"That's better."

He began maneuvering me out of my attack and into defense more than I wanted to be, making me think harder to get back on the attack. We continued battling until he decided we were done, at which point he put me on my back. I didn't get up right away. I closed my eyes, breathing hard. I was annoyed that he put me on my back. I knew he was better than I, and that I had practiced long before he showed up, but in my head, there was no excuse.

I mentally took notes of all that had occurred, and realized he hadn't said *dead*. I took one last deep breath, and pushed myself back up with my sword swinging. I caught a glimpse of his surprise before he smiled at his mistake.

He dodged my strike, my blade barely missing him. He swung himself around as I moved into my next attack and our blades clanked. After ten more moves, I heard the dreaded word.

119

"Dead," he breathed in my ear.

He moved his sword away from my neck and let go of the wrist that held my blade, but he didn't release me. His hand slid onto my stomach, holding me close to him.

Part of me was glad that he didn't release me completely because I was sure that I would have fallen to the ground if he had. That was the most intense session I had ever had with Alex. And even though I was dead, there was a strong sense of confidence that was circulating within me.

"That was quick thinking," he remarked, breathing harder than normal.

I smiled as he slowly let go of me. It took all my strength to not sag to the ground. I turned around ready to make a snide comment, but I completely lost my train of thought.

"Alex, you're bleeding!" I exclaimed as I moved closer. I moved his shirt away from his side to see the blood flowing from the wound. "I'm so sorry."

"It's my fault for underestimating… I should know better," he smiled, but I did not.

"We should head back and clean it up," I said, not hiding how awful I felt. My blade hadn't ever come even close to scratching him in any of our previous training sessions. I shifted my eyes to his face to see that he wasn't the least bit upset. How could he not be upset?!

"It'll be okay. It isn't the first, and it's far from the worst," he commented, his eyes not looking away from mine.

"I appreciate you trying to make me not feel bad…"

"You shouldn't," he said in a serious tone. "This means you're ready for the Tournament."

I shook my head. The cut must have been deep because the blood was continuing to soak his shirt.

"Come on, Alex, let's get back," I stated, suddenly not caring about the Tournament. My eyes searched our surroundings and realized I had no idea where we were. "Which way are we supposed to go?"

"Sonia, relax," Alex said in his calm voice, and I heard a hint of laughter. "I'm going to be fine, won't even leave a scar."

"Look at your side," I replied, not understanding his amusement. "I more than just grazed you."

"It's just blood."

"It's not supposed to be on the outside."

"Okay, grab your sword," he calmly said, still smiling.

My sword? I hadn't even realized that I had dropped it. As I saw it laying on the ground, I quickly picked it up and slid it into its sheath on my back. I turned back around to see Alex leaning against the tree with his sword sheathed on his back and I ran over to him.

"Alex," I whispered as I touched him. His eyes opened and he smiled affectionately at me. "Can you walk?"

"It's really not bad," he assured me. I grabbed the arm that was on the same side as his wound, and pulled it around my shoulder. I put my other arm around his waist, and we started walking.

"I am so sorry," I continued to apologize as we walked back home. His body seemed tense, and I was sure he was angry. How had I…

"Phillip isn't going to be as good as me," Alex began as if I hadn't injured him. "If you can take that energy you found right there at the end, you might just win."

I let him go on about how I could win the Tournament, but I was sure that I didn't want to tap into that energy again. I wounded Alex, and still couldn't remember when it had happened. I just wanted to get him home, and have Krissy clean up his wound.

"Sonia, you're not listening to me," Alex stated, his voice cutting into my thoughts. "The Tournament is in three days, you need to be focused."

"I will focus after Krissy cleans your injury."

"I guess this will cure her thoughts that I am being indecent with you," he replied with humor.

"Alex, this isn't funny."

"I don't think I've ever seen you like this," he commented.

"I don't remember hitting you, and you're bleeding profusely."

"In the last two weeks, you've proved that the Tournament is your passion, nothing has swayed you…"

"I've never wounded you before," I replied. I couldn't believe that it didn't bother him.

He stopped walking, and I glimpsed up at his face. He was staring at me in astonishment, his eyes searching mine.

"I'm okay," he assured me.

I knew I should be proud of myself at being able to wound Alex, but I wasn't. I felt horrible. I glanced down at my feet and his fingers came under my chin, moving my face back up so that I would look at him. I didn't understand why he wasn't angry or annoyed or anything but calm and...

His eyes gazed deep into mine and my thoughts faded away. I was sure his face was moving closer to mine. It didn't even occur to me that I...

Alex's head moved up abruptly, and I watched his face become very serious before I heard the footsteps. I quickly turned around to see Phillip standing there. Phillip's attention was on Alex, but as his eyes fell upon me he smiled.

"What are you doing here?" I cautiously inquired. "Father doesn't..."

"Your sister said you were practicing out here, so I thought I'd check out my competition," he smoothly replied. "My father, as much as he hates to admit it, believes that you'll be the best I'll come up against." He stepped closer and I watched his eyes flit over to Alex and then back to me. He glanced at my left shoulder, "I see you've even acquired a sword. May I see it?"

I was about to say yes, but I suddenly became annoyed that he hadn't even noticed that his uncle was bleeding. He was holding us up when Alex needed to get to the house.

123

"No," I answered curtly, and astonishment filled his face. I turned back around and continued to walk with Alex, focusing in the direction of the house. I glanced up at Alex to see he was staring at me in surprise, and I quickly focused in the direction we needed to go.

"Alex, there's a lot of talk going on," he started nonchalantly.

I stopped in my tracks. Had Krissy sent him out here?! I turned to face him. "We don't care," I growled. Phillip's eyes fixed on Alex and I turned back towards the house.

"She's of age, Alex. No one will…" Phillip began.

Alex moved so quickly, by the time I turned around Alex had his sword at Phillip's neck. He spoke to Philip in a quiet growl and Phillip answered in the same tone with a scowl. I wasn't sure if it was because they were speaking in growling tones, but I did not understand anything that was being said between them.

Phillip smiled as he glanced over at me. His lips continued moving as his face became arrogant. He stopped talking abruptly, his eyes focused back on Alex and I assumed that it was because Alex had interrupted him. Fear rose into Phillip's eyes, and I wondered what Alex had said.

Finally Alex dropped his sword away from Phillip's neck, but Phillip didn't move. "Get out of here," Alex said, but it sounded more like a fierce growl and Alex's demeanor sent a chill through me.

I couldn't ever remember seeing Alex behave in such a way.

Phillip hastily moved away from Alex. He glanced at me with a smile of desire, and disappeared into the trees.

"Come Sonia, we need to get you home," Alex sternly said, without a glance in my direction.

Needed to get *me* home? I normally would have said something to him, but by his tone I knew it was better to keep quiet.

Alex sheathed his sword and started to walk as though I wasn't there. I hurried to his side, wanting to know what was going on. I reached up and touched his arm, but he quickly side stepped away from me. I stared at him with concern, he felt warmer than he should have, and I felt fear's grip tighten on me. What did I do to him? Was it because of the metal he insisted Percy use?

"Alex?"

He didn't answer. Alex seemed very focused on our destination. Had Phillip taunted Alex about being injured by me? Was Alex angry that *I* had wounded him? The last thing I ever wanted to do was make Alex look bad in front of anyone. I glanced down at his blood soaked shirt, the guilt was overwhelming.

"Alex, is everything okay?"

His eyes finally focused on me, and his face softened a little. There was a powerful look in his eyes that I had never seen before, and I didn't know if I should be in awe or afraid. I reached out for him, and again he kept himself just out of reach.

125

Something was desperately wrong, but I wasn't sure what it was. I let my hand fall back to my side and stopped walking. I continued to stare at him, expecting him to keep walking and leave me alone in the woods. He normally would never leave me alone, but this didn't feel normal. He stopped two steps ahead of me and turned so that he was facing me. I shifted my attention to my feet waiting for him to say something, waiting for the parental tone that would enrage me.

"We should get back to the house," he whispered and I nodded, but I didn't move. He took a step closer to me. "Sonia," he softly said. There was something in his tone that I hadn't heard before, and I glanced up at him. "Walk with me," he requested, and after a moment's hesitation I took a step. He waited until I was next to him before he began walking again.

We slowly walked the rest of the way in silence. I didn't fail to notice that he didn't look at me and continued to stay a short distance away. He started walking faster once the house was in sight, and I hurried to keep up with him. Alex walked up to the house and stopped in front of the door. I halted as I saw the blood on his shirt that was now soaking into his pants, and remembered that I need to get Krissy to fix the injury that I had caused.

How had I gotten so caught up with how Alex was acting when he had every right to be distant from me? He pushed the door open, and I quickly ran to catch up to him. As soon as I was inside, I realized that no one was home.

Where was Father and Krissy?

Alex walked into the kitchen and I hurried into the bathroom, wishing I had paid more attention to all the times I watched Krissy patching people up. I grabbed the box of bandages, one bowl, and two towels. I turned and filled the bowl with hot water before quickly walking to the kitchen. I opened the door to find Alex in a chair, slumped over the table.

I hurried over to the table and I put my stuff down, glancing over at him. His eyes were closed, but his face was filled with tension.

"Alex," I called softly.

He lifted his head, and I helped him sit back. How was his temperature still rising?! I grabbed his shirt, pulled it over his head, and knelt down next to him. His eyes opened as I touched his bare torso.

"Sonia," he quietly said. "I need to go."

"You're not going anywhere right now, Alex. I need to…"

"It's not that bad. It's important that I…"

What had I done to him? His skin was too hot. I quickly grabbed the bowl of water and a towel. I started washing off his side, and my breath caught. It was a thin, deep gouge across his side, the best I was going to be able to do was tape it. If it ever stopped bleeding. Why wasn't Krissy here?!

"Sonia," he started again.

"I'm not going to let you leave until I clean this up. This is my fault," I began, my concern loud in my voice.

"It's not your fault," he sternly argued. "But I do have to go."

127

As his eyes met mine, he stopped talking. I couldn't look away from him. The power in his eyes was mesmerizing.

"Sonia," he said again, pulling me up as he stood.

His hand brushed along my face. His touch was overly warm, but I didn't stop gazing into his eyes.

"I have to go now," he whispered, but I felt as though he didn't want to go.

In fact, I was sure that his face was moving closer to mine. He breathed in deep and I closed my eyes, wanting him to hold me close. The heat from his hand emanated onto my cheek, and the warmth began to move through me. His hand abruptly moved away and when I opened my eyes he was gone.

CHAPTER TWELVE

What just happened?

"Alex?"

I glanced around the empty kitchen, not sure what I should be doing. Why did I feel so lost all of a sudden?

I had to get out of here, away from this feeling. I hurried outside, hoping Alex would be there - he would make it better. I frantically searched for him, but he wasn't anywhere. I ran around the house to the stable, and saw that Storm was still there.

Where did Alex go? He never left without Storm. I put my hands on my head, trying to calm my mind. I began to walk over to Storm, not understanding what was happening. I abruptly turned, I had to find Alex. I quickly exited the stable, trying to pull my thoughts together.

His skin was so hot…and his eyes… What was it about his eyes? How could they radiate so much power? There had been an invisible force pulling me to him - I had felt it.

Storm walked next to me, lowering his head to my shoulder. I stopped walking as I absently placed my hand on his nose, and rested my head against him.

Phillip. What had transpired between him and Phillip? Alex wasn't angry until Phillip had shown up.

Storm neighed, and I moved away from him. "I don't know where he went," I said. "Away from me, I guess."

I patted Storm's neck, and distractedly walked away. I shouldn't care that he left - he always came and went when he wanted - but I wanted him here with me. I heard Storm following me, and I stopped. I glimpsed over my shoulder surprised to see him right behind me. He lowered his head and neighed softly.

"I'm just going to walk. You can come with me, if you like," I quietly said, certain that he wouldn't.

I shifted my eyes towards the road and began walking. I was astounded that Storm continued to follow me, maybe he didn't like that Alex had disappeared without him. We walked together towards the road. Maybe I'd go into town, and see what was going on. I hadn't been there in a long time. Plus, I was curious about the Arena and...

The sound of hooves pounding the ground caused me to look up. I couldn't tell who was riding, but a bad feeling raced through me. Storm started stomping his feet on the ground, and I anxiously glanced at him. His posture did not relax me. I glimpsed back at the house which was a small square in the distance. I turned to start running back home, but Storm moved in front of me and neighed loudly.

I stared up at him in surprise. Was he blocking me from returning to the house? Storm neighed with urgency. What did he…

He was expecting me to get up on him? "But Alex said…"

Storm neighed again, moving his nose towards his back. He *did* want me on his back. I glanced back at the riders, and shook my head at how fast they were traveling. I sure hope I was right about Storm wanting me on him. I focused on Storm, trying to remain calm. How was I going to get up on his back?

"Let me get a running start, maybe I can get up there," I said to him, not sounding confident.

I backed up several feet away, and ran to him. I jumped up towards the horse's back and almost made it. I held tight to his mane and got my leg over him. I quickly situated myself, wrapping my fingers in his mane, and he immediately took off running. I glanced behind me to see that they were now closer to us than we were to the house.

They couldn't be men from town - no one owned horses that fast. How were we going to make it to the house in time? They were larger than any man I had ever seen, and their horses continued to gain. I had a horrible feeling that home was not going to be a safe place to go.

I glanced back again, they were almost upon us. My fears were rising - I didn't know what to do. Panic was making it hard to think.

What if Father or Krissy came back?

There was a roar from above and I instantly began to search the sky, already knowing what it was. The black dragon was diving towards whoever was after me. The dragon grabbed two of the riders with the long toes of his front feet. He flung them in the direction that they had come and dove after them. There were three riders left, and they were closing in on us.

Storm turned sharply away from the house, almost knocking me off. He began running for the woods, and I glanced behind me to see they were still trailing us, but Storm had put a little more distance between us and them. The dragon soared in, and grabbed two more riders. I unsheathed my sword, knowing that the dragon wasn't going to get back to us in time. I pulled Storm's mane, and the horse halted.

"Let's not run from this guy," I aggressively said as I unsheathed my sword.

Storm neighed loudly and turned. I held my sword above my head as we attacked. I swung my sword as we moved next to him, causing the rider to fall off. I quickly slid off of Storm who hadn't stopped running, and Storm neighed irritably. As soon as my feet hit the ground, I was running towards him… it.

It was not a man I was up against, but instead a creature that I hadn't ever seen or heard of before - not even in stories. It was covered in armor, but the skin that was barely showing between the plates was an ugly green, and it had…*three* eyes? I swallowed hard, and tightened the grip on my sword. I couldn't change my mind now, there wasn't time.

I swung my sword, and the blade cut across the creature's side. Its eyes intensified and it brought its hand up. It wasn't the extraordinary large hand that bothered me, but the two-sided axe the hand was holding that made the fear surge through me. It swung the axe down towards me and I dove away from it, rolling across the ground to get out of its way. I quickly got to my feet only to find the creature standing in front of me again.

I swung my sword as it lifted the axe over its head. The tip of my blade scraped across the space on his chest that wasn't covered by his armor. This time it yelled a startling sound, and without hesitation I began to run. The creature grabbed me, and threw me through the air. I hit the ground, rolling to a stop face down.

It took me a second to remember that my life was in danger and I needed to get my body moving. As I looked up, I saw the woods. I hastily got to my feet and sprinted for the trees, I could lose him in there. Storm neighed loudly, he actually sounded furious. The creature made an awful sound, but I didn't waste a moment to see what was going on.

I had just entered into the trees when a hand wrap around the back of my neck, forcing me against a tree so hard that the bark cut into my face.

I waited for the hand to let go so that I could fight back. As I was released, I turned with my sword leading. A hand came around my wrist that held my sword, and swung me into another tree deeper into the forest.

"You haven't learned yet?" Marty hissed as his forearm pressed against the back of my neck before my body had a chance to fall to the ground. His handed clamped onto my left wrist, and I cried out in pain, but refused to let go of my sword.

I struggled against him, but it was useless. He let up the pressure on my neck, allowing my body to move away from the tree. I had every intention of attacking him, but he slammed me up against the tree again. The bark cut deeply into my face and my blood instantly began flowing.

"I don't understand what my brother is waiting for. Your life is over," Marty snarled in my ear.

I heard the growl of the Shadow at the edge of the trees.

"He's too angry to save you, Sonia."

He slammed my body against the tree again. This time the bark of the tree cut into my chest, and a cry of pain escaped my lips. He turned me to face him before releasing me. I moved away from the tree preparing to attack him, but he moved faster. His hand hit my bleeding chest with so much force that when I hit the tree behind me, it took my breath away and I crumbled to the ground, dropping my sword.

"He's only delaying the inevitable," he sneered as he stepped next to my unmoving body.

I was fighting for my breath. Tears filled my eyes as I realized I couldn't get back up. Marty rolled me over with his foot, causing me to cry out. I stared up at him and he smiled maliciously as he crouched down next to me.

"Pathetic. I think that if he isn't going to take you, then it's up to us. You're not my type, but Phillip has taken quite an interest in you. He's more than willing to do what my brother has not." His attention shifted to the direction I had last heard the dragon and smiled deviously before he continued. "Yes, I will let Phillip do what he does best."

The dragon roared ferociously, and panic began to race through me.

"I look forward to seeing Phillip put you in your place," he whispered with a smile, and I screamed as the blade I didn't see cut along my side. "Although, it won't be at the Tournament."

The dragon roared fiercely, and Marty held up a short blade that was coated with my blood. I thought I saw red flash in his eyes as the dragon roared again, but I wasn't sure. Marty clenched his jaw and stood up, staring deep into the forest as though he were concentrating on a new puzzle.

The Shadow roared with such ferocity this time that the world trembled in fear. Marty's face snapped in the dragon's direction, his whole demeanor expressed his unease. I watched him calm himself before he looked down and smiled at me. He held the bloody blade between us and began to bend closer to me.

"Yes, Phillip will…" he began as he moved his blade towards my chest, but stopped as he suddenly turned away from me.

135

I heard Storm neighing angrily as his hooves beat against the ground. I saw fear on Marty's face before his eyes shifted back down to me. He took a moment to stare at me in disgust, as though I was worthless, before he disappeared.

I closed my eyes to fight against the tears that wanted to slide down my face. My injuries were making it hard to breathe, and the pain was overriding my ability to focus. Something nudged my body, startling me, and I opened my eyes. Storm lowered his head next to mine and breathed hard on me. I put my trembling hand up and touched his chin. I forced myself to rollover, trying to will myself to get up, but I couldn't summon the energy.

The dragon roared again, but not as ferociously, and Storm made a strange noise back. The dragon made a rumbling noise that wasn't as loud. The horse whinnied back.

They were talking to each other? How could a horse speak with a dragon?

After a few moments of quiet, Storm nudged the side of my face.

"I'll be okay," I said unconvincingly. I attempted to get up again, but I just couldn't do it.

I wanted to cry. The Tournament was only three days away, and my wrist was fractured at best, I couldn't even make a fist with it. I didn't want to begin to wonder what might be wrong with my ribcage. I continued to lay there with my face bleeding into the dirt, wondering what I had done to make Marty despise me so much.

I finally turned my head toward Storm as he softly whinnied. To my amazement the horse had laid down next to me. I reached for my sword with my good hand and felt the blade graze my shoulder as I slid it awkwardly into the sheath. The blood slowly moved over my shoulder, but it was nothing compared to how my body felt.

I closed my eyes for a moment, trying to calm my mind as panic and misery attempted to overwhelm me. I couldn't move my body off the ground, and with my luck the Ortal were on their way.

I opened my eyes, and watched as Storm maneuvered himself so that he was leaning in my direction and his mane fell across my uninjured hand. I tightened my fingers into a fist, and very carefully Storm rolled onto his stomach, pulling me onto his back. I cringed at the pain in my ribs, stifling the scream of pain, and keeping my fist tight. No matter what, I was not going to let go his mane. I knew this was my only chance to get out of here.

Storm moved slowly as he stood. I tried to move myself into a sitting position, but I couldn't bear the pain. I continued to hold on, and fought the desire to close my eyes, afraid that I would never open them again. I watched the trees pass by, and was surprised at how smoothly Storm maneuvered through the forest. He was truly a magnificent animal. As he walked out of the trees and back towards the road, I saw the orange sky of the setting sun.

137

My eye lids were getting heavier and Storm started running faster as though he knew I couldn't hold on much longer. I focused on the orange of the sky. The orbs of fire burst from my memory, and I shook my head. Tears began to slide from my eyes, and I found myself wishing the dragon had killed me in the Batwas Valley.

I tried not to think about anything because I was certain that I wouldn't be able to stop crying. My eyes closed with the weight of my agony, but still I fought to stay conscious. Gentle hands slid on my torso, carefully sliding my body off the horse. I knew it wasn't my father because there was no yelling.

"Oh no," Alex whispered. A small gasp of pain escaped my lips as he rolled my broken body over to carry me in his arms.

I opened my eyes to see Alex's face hidden in shadows. My anger surged through me as I thought about the hurry he had been in to leave earlier. Is *that* what Phillip had told him? Were they *all* against me? Was this some kind of cruel joke? If I could have moved my body, I would have run far away from him.

He opened the door and as the light hit his face, I was surprised at the amount of blood that covered him. All of my anger washed away as I wondered what had happened to him.

He took me up the stairs and into his room. He carefully laid me on the bed. He lifted my shirt, and I screamed as his fingers moved along my ribs.

Tears flooded down my cheeks, burning into the wounds on my face.

"I'll be right back," he assured me before he disappeared.

I blinked the tears out of my eyes as I tried to ignore the pain. Today was over. In two days the tournament would begin and I...

"I'm going to have to clean these wounds," he apologized.

What was the point?

His bloody face was sad and rueful, and I hastily focused on the ceiling. Something had definitely happened to him. His shirt was shredded and his arms and chest were as bloody as his face. He didn't even seem to notice or care about the wounds that he had.

"I think that Krissy and your father went to town already."

I didn't respond. I was glad that they were safe.

"With a good night's rest, most of this should be fine in the morning."

He apparently didn't notice my wrist or...

He began wiping my face and whatever he was cleaning my wounds with stung horribly, silencing my thoughts. Alex reached over me to the table on the other side of the bed and turned on the light. He quickly moved back and placed a warm cloth on my face that soothed the pain on my face.

He started to apologize again, and I shook my head at him. This wasn't his fault. This was Marty trying to prevent me from competing in the

139

Tournament. I became angry at the thought that he might have accomplished it this time.

Alex put the cloth down, and his eyes scanned my body. He pulled out a dagger and sliced through the leather band that held my sheath to my back. He pulled the sheath out from underneath me, and I watched him lean it against his bed.

He ripped the material of my shirt on my shoulder and wiped gel into the wound that I had created when I sheathed my sword. As a burning sensation overwhelmed the pain, I quickly focused on Alex's face that he still hadn't cleaned up. I didn't see any gouges and realized that the blood on Alex's face wasn't his.

Had he been fighting too?

I grabbed his hand with my good hand, and he stopped tending to me. After a moment he gazed down at me. His eyes focused on mine, and I could see how sad he was.

"Thank you," I whispered.

"You need to rest," he softly replied, with a shake of his head.

I shook my head. I was too afraid that if I closed my eyes I wouldn't wake up until after the Tournament… and he would be gone.

He leaned in close, and whispered something into my ear that I didn't understand. I felt his cheek skim mine, causing a warm sensation to move through me before sleep took over.

CHAPTER THIRTEEN

I awoke to find that I was still in Alex's room. I did a mental check of my body. Everything felt good. I lifted the wrist that Marty had injured to see a white bandage around it. I took a deep breath preparing myself for the worst, but as I opened and closed my fingers there wasn't any pain, and I sighed with relief.

I sat up quickly as panic raced through me. The Tournament!

"How are you?" Alex asked.

I turned my head to see that Alex was sitting in a chair by the bed, smiling. It wasn't his usual smile, but he did seem relieved.

"The Tournament…" I started.

"You've got time," he calmly replied.

I relaxed and moved my legs off the bed. I stood up the same time Alex did and we were standing toe to toe. I glanced up at him as he tilted his face down. I could feel his eyes staring deep into my soul, and I completely stopped thinking about the Tournament. I wanted to run my finger over a cut that was on his forehead. He must have acquired…

"You can use my sheath," he said, bringing my mind back into focus.

141

"Thank you," I quietly replied, looking away from his face, remembering that he cut mine off of me.

"Go get changed, and then we'll take Storm into town," he said in the calm voice that, as a child, always soothed me.

I nodded, not looking at him this time. Something inside of me felt very different today - like clarity, but I didn't know about what. I glanced at Alex as I neared the door, searching his face for an answer. He smiled kindly and I smiled back before I turned and ran down the stairs. I was surprised at how good I felt. Alex definitely was good at healing. I wondered what it was that he used.

I walked into my room and over to my dresser. I began pulling out a change of clothes when I heard the door close.

"So, now are you still going to tell me that there is nothing going on between you and Alex?" Krissy bitterly inquired.

I turned and could feel my anger surge through me as if our last conversation hadn't ended. I bit my tongue, reminding myself that it didn't matter what she thought.

"Well?"

"Well what? I have a Tournament to get to," I stated in a controlled calm as I started to change. I noticed that Alex had taped up my side, leaving all my other injuries to heal on their own. There were several cuts across my chest, and I pushed on my sternum. I was relieved when my chest did not ache at all.

"Seriously, Sonia! You've been up in his room for two days."

"I was unconscious. Do you really think that Alex would take advantage of me?" I inquired as calmly as I could, pulling my shirt over my head.

"He only came down twice, briefly. I heard him telling dad that you were *healing* again, but he was alone with you the majority of the time. I offered to go up, but he and Father both wouldn't allow it."

I hid my surprise at that information. Why wouldn't they allow Krissy to…

"Phillip came by a few days ago." The mention of his name caused fear and more anger. "I let him in and we talked for a while. He seemed concerned about you. I met him in town the other night, and he came over again last night. He is very handsome *and* charming. He…"

"…is my competition," I growled.

"He tried to talk with father about you until Alex came downstairs. Alex grabbed Phillip by the arm as if Phillip was a child, and pulled him outside."

"Well, Phillip *is* a child to Alex. Alex is his uncle," I informed her.

She went on as if what Alex had done was unnecessary and she herself was insulted.

"Again, he is my competition," I reminded her, unable to hide my irritation.

I finished getting dressed and headed for the door, but she stepped in front of me.

"Well, I snuck out the window so that I could move closer to hear them talking. Phillip told Alex that Marty doesn't understand what Alex is doing,

143

but Alex needed to make a choice. But before Phillip had a chance to say anything more, Alex stood tall over him and told Phillip that he had better leave you alone. Phillip cowered a little… but who wouldn't have, Alex is quite intimidating when he's angry…" she paused and I stepped around her. "Or jealous."

I stopped walking toward the door and turned to glare at her.

"It's totally understandable. Phillip is much more attractive and closer to your age. I realize that Alex doesn't appear that much older anymore, but with the amount of time that he's been in our lives he has to be closer to father's age than yours. You should think things through a little better."

My jaw hit the floor. She *wanted* me to be interested in a guy, and she'd prefer it was Phillip?

"You don't agree? Because Phillip told Alex that after this competition, things were going to change, and that Alex was treading on dangerous land. Phillip went on about Marty for a moment, but I wasn't listening. I was watching Alex become furious. He said something that I didn't understand and Phillip returned a comment that I didn't hear correctly. Alex took a step towards Phillip and Phillip backed away into the shadows.

"So, if nothing is going on between you and Alex, then what was that show of dominance for?"

"Phillip isn't to be trusted," I stated, wondering if she had made it all up.

"Did Alex tell you that? I've seen the way Alex looks at you."

What was she talking about?

"No. Alex did not tell me that," I replied. "I just have a bad feeling about Phillip."

"I don't know how that is possible. He's perfect in *every* way."

"Maybe I don't trust him because he's my competition, and he keeps trying to get close to me, as if he was trying to cheat. Or *maybe* it's because Marty is his father and Marty has been trying to remove me from this Tournament."

"Whatever. If I were you, I'd let Phillip win this little competition and…"

"And thank goodness you're not…" I quickly bit my tongue, and left the room.

What had gotten into her? I knew she was envious of the attention that Alex was giving me, but that conversation was so ridiculous. If I hadn't known any better I would have thought the girl in that room wasn't Krissy. Everything about her seemed off, including her posture and tone of voice.

I didn't have time for this. I shook my head, and walked outside to see Alex and my father talking. My father nodded, "I trust you Alex. Do what you think is right, just keep her safe."

"Father, don't worry about me," I said as I walked up to them.

They both turned and smiled at me.

"Ready to go?" Alex inquired as he leapt onto Storm.

I gave my father a hug, and ran my hand down Storm's face before I nodded at Alex. I noticed that he had his sword sheathed behind him and that my sword along with several other things were packed

145

up on Storm behind Alex. He leaned down and pulled me up, setting me down in front of him.

"Are you okay?" he whispered as his arm wrapped around me.

"Quite," I replied curtly, thinking about how Phillip was speaking with my sister.

That was the last thing we said to each other until we arrived in town a few hours later. After I shoved Krissy and Phillip out of my mind, my fears of the Tournament surfaced. I couldn't have held a conversation if I wanted to. My stomach was twisted into knots, and the closer we got to town the more I wondered if this was such a good idea.

Women hardly ever entered, and only one woman had come close to the final match. It shouldn't have meant anything to me, because a lot of men never made it to the final match. And no one had the trainer that I did, and few had the obsession that I felt about winning. Most people just wanted to win for the glory or the money. I didn't want to be exalted and I didn't want the money. I just wanted to win.

We rode through town where people from all over were gathering. Alex pointed out people from the other side of the Batwas Valley, from the mountains, and beyond. I knew the world was bigger than just Lord Vertas' land, but until now I hadn't realized just how small his land was. The land that we lived on covered a great distance, but apparently the world was bigger than I had dreamed it was.

I saw the boys that I trained with ahead of us, and others I had seen around town over the years.

None were happy to see me and their glaring screamed their dislike of me.

"They're just frustrated because they know that their chances of winning have disappeared," Alex whispered cheerfully in my ear.

I nodded. That was probably true, but at the moment I wasn't so sure. I continued to look among the people gathering. My stomach tightened more as I realized that I had only seen a couple of other female opponents. Some of which were very intimidating. They appeared stronger and bigger than the men, while others were visually distracting to the men. I glanced over my shoulder at Alex who didn't even seem to notice them.

He was focused in a whole different direction. As he nodded his head, I followed his gaze to where he was looking. There was a small group of men that I was confident lived in Lord Vertas' castle. Their armor was flawless and it did not appear as though they had ever seen any hardship.

I suddenly became aware that people were taking notice of us as we neared them. They stopped what they were doing to turn and get a better look. I watched jaws drop while others stared and talked to each other - their eyes never leaving Alex and I. I quickly focused on Storm's mane as my stomach tightened even more. I no longer wanted to notice anything else.

When we finally stopped, we were at the outdoor Arena. There was a strange echo coming from the direction of the Arena and I was certain that people must have already begun to fill the stands.

My hands tightened in Storm's mane as my mind shut off.

"Don't worry, this will be over in two days," Alex said with humor.

I just nodded that I understood, and he laughed.

All this training and I really hadn't given much thought to what it was going to be like fighting in front of all these people. I had watched the Tournament twice with Alex, and not once did I think about how it would feel to have a thousand people watching.

Alex dismounted and Storm followed close to him. I heard a couple of cat calls, but was too nervous to shift my eyes away from Storm's mane. I held tight to Storm, not caring anymore about what the Arena looked like or who all was going to fight or watch. I didn't even glance up when Storm stopped walking.

"Sonia," Alex's calm voice finally interrupted my growing anxiety.

I tore my eyes away from Storm and glanced towards Alex's voice. I saw him smiling, and I forced myself to smile back. He held his arms up for me to slide down into. I stared at him for a moment, debating what to do. I quickly threw my left leg over Storm's back, and slid off before I could stop myself.

I was glad that Alex had been standing there because my legs did not support me. Instead of his arms just softening my drop, I ended up embraced in his arms.

"I can't do this," I whispered into his chest.

"Yes, you can," he whispered back, his lips next to my forehead.

"I can't even stand right now. I don't even know if I can hold my blade," I blurted out nervously as I closed my eyes. "I'm sorry, Alex."

His fingers slid under my chin and tilted my face up. I didn't want to look at him. I was foolish and naïve to believe that I could do this.

"I can't," I said again, shaking my head. He gently tucked my hair behind my ear, causing me to gaze upon his face.

"Let's practice," he said. "It'll relax you."

I slowly nodded. He continued to hold me close to him as he reached over my head and grabbed my sword.

His eyes met mine, and the strength that I saw in them began to move through me. His arm slid away from me as he slowly stepped away. "Don't forget to breathe," he quietly said.

I glanced up blankly to see he was smiling at me in a comforting way, like he always did when I was afraid of something that I shouldn't be.

Again I nodded. He handed me my sword, and I wrapped my fingers around the handle. I braced for the pain to shoot up my arm, but it didn't. I immediately glimpsed at Alex and he took his high guard. I shook off my surprise, and lifted my sword. I closed my eyes and breathed for a minute. I opened them and focused on Alex before starting a slow attack.

He didn't get frustrated at me for not moving quicker or hitting harder. He just followed my

149

tempo, and soon I began to relax and move faster. After a little while longer we were moving fluidly together like we had a million times before. I watched him smile as I came in close for a daring hit. Of course, he blocked it.

"Dead," he whispered into my ear a few hits later, causing goose bumps to race down my body.

I took a small step away from him and slowly turned to face him. He was staring at me with fondness and I met his eyes, trying to understand the sensation that was going through me.

"So you were able to get her here after all."

Marty's voice startled me, and Alex took a step away from me and closer to Marty. What was he doing here?

"You looked awfully nervous coming in, Sonia," Marty said, moving so he could see around Alex. Marty's eyes shifted back to Alex before he continued. "I told you your time is almost up."

"Sonia, why don't you take a break, and watch the fight in the Arena," Alex suggested in a serious tone without a glance in my direction.

My eyes flitted to Marty who was smirking at me, and anger instead of fear raced through me. I walked over to Storm to sheath my sword, taking in the room that Alex and I were in. It wasn't huge, but there was enough room to practice. There were two beds and an alcove for Storm. Two beds... We were going to sleep in here too?

"Take it with you," Alex said from behind me.

Alex moved in front of me and strapped his sheath onto my back. I glanced up as he finished tightening it. His eyes shifted to mine and his face softened. He took my sword from my hand and sheathed it over my back.

"I'll come find you in a few minutes," he assured me.

I nodded at Alex, not wanting to look away from him. Alex tore his eyes away from me before quickly turning back toward Marty.

I turned toward the door and headed out, not understanding what it was that felt different between Alex and I, but I knew that something had changed. I shook my head. It probably wasn't anything except my nerves. I would win the Tournament and everything would go back to normal.

As I walked away I realized every fighter had a room designated for them down the same hallway. It was like a giant stable, but more comfortable.

Most everyone I saw seemed to have jitters about the upcoming fights. I didn't see anyone sitting as I walked passed the open doors of each room. They were pacing, practicing, or jumping up and down, trying to release the pressure and fears that came with wanting to win.

I walked down the dim hallway toward the Arena where cheers and foul language were bursting into the air. I stepped into the sunlight and walked to a fence that held the other fighters back from the main fight. I leaned my elbows on the wooden fence, and felt the memories of my childhood surge into my mind.

I remembered how Alex always had to hold me tight because I was so excited about watching the

151

Tournament, and he was afraid I'd get lost. He would put me on his shoulders so that I could have a good seat and see the whole fight. He would sometimes explain the battle to me, but he usually waited until it was finished before he'd go over the fight and tell me the flaws and strengths of the warriors that had battled. I loved the way he talked about the fight to me. The way he...

"Checking out the competition?" Phillip asked, interrupting my memories.

I side glanced at him. He was standing too close to me, and I took a step to the side away from him. I quickly focused back on the Arena, keeping my eyes on the battle in front of me.

"Just because Alex and my father don't get along, doesn't mean we can't," he commented in a charming manner.

"My sister doesn't seem to mind that my father or Alex don't particularly care for you. Why don't you go and talk with her," I curtly said.

"Your sister...? Oh yes, Krissy," he said in such a way that I looked over at him with irritation. He smiled handsomely and continued, "She does not approve of the attention that Alex gives you."

I rolled my eyes and shifted my attention back at the fight. "She just hates the fact that *a* guy is paying attention to me instead of her."

"Well she should get used to it. You have a natural beauty that she cannot compete with, and if guys weren't intimidated by you, you'd have quite a selection."

"I'm not looking for a selection."

"So, Alex is your pick then?"

"Alex is my trainer, my father's friend."

"Not yours?"

"Of course he's my friend," I retorted with irritation. I just hadn't realized that I had gotten old enough that our age difference allowed him to be my friend and not just my father's.

"Well, if he's your *friend*, then you're not tied to him."

"I will not be *tied* to anyone, ever," I said in a serious tone. "So, since that is obviously what you're looking for, let me save you the time. Don't come near me again."

He grabbed my bicep as I attempted to leave, turning me to face him. He smiled and started to open his mouth when he suddenly turned his head. He quickly focused back on me and something malicious flashed in his eyes, reminding me of Marty. He abruptly pulled me close to him, rubbing his cheek against mine.

"Let the competition begin," he whispered in my ear and pressed his lips against mine.

I swung my fist and made contact with his face. He just continued to smile with a devious gleam in his eye and disappeared into the crowd as everyone stood and cheered.

I was going to drive my sword through that snake.

"Sorry I couldn't get here... What's wrong?" Alex asked as he stepped close.

"Nothing," I growled, staring at the vacant ground of the Arena. The winner and loser of the match had already been removed, and I had missed it.

"You're up soon," he said, stepping away from me suddenly distracted. "Let's get you ready."

I felt my mouth go dry, and the whole world stopped moving. Alex chuckled and gently wrapped his hand around my arm, walking me back to our room.

He pulled the bag off of Storm and opened it. "This should protect you from the blades," he said, holding up a very tight looking leather-type outfit.

"What?" Was he serious? He expected me to wear that?

"This is much lighter than what the others will most likely be wearing. It won't hinder your moves like the traditional armor, and it's not nearly as bad as it looks," he said humorously.

"That's not going to fit me," I replied, shaking my head.

"It will, and it will protect you from even Phillip's blade. So long as he abides by the rules," he informed me. "It does have a few weak spots, but with the way you fight I don't think we need to worry."

He walked over to me, removed his sheath from my back, and slid the armor over my head. I immediately slid my arms into the sleeves, as Alex finished pulling it down and began fastening the edges together. I was impressed, it had slipped on easier than I had expected. It was like slipping into my favorite pajamas. It didn't squish me at all, and I could move around freely.

"See, I told you," he smiled, and replaced the sheath on my back.

"Thank you, Alex," I said, beaming from ear to ear.

"There is better stuff out there, but this will do for the Tournament," he replied nonchalantly.

"How did you…"

"Percy," he interrupted. "He saw more than he meant, and told me that I had better have this for you."

"I will pay you back after I win," I smiled.

"It's from Percy," he said again.

It probably was from Percy, but he paid for it. I glanced up to continue to argue with him, but my mind lost its train of thought. There was an odd expression on his face… almost sad.

"Alex, is your fighter ready?" asked a rough voice I didn't recognize before I had a chance to ask Alex what was wrong.

No, I thought. I hesitantly shifted my eyes away from Alex to see a short man standing in the entrance.

"Yes," Alex replied.

"Take her to the Arena," the stocky man said and turned to leave, but he quickly turned back towards us and took strides that should have been too long for his short legs. When he was standing before us, he shifted his attention to Alex. "Marty toyed with the list, and weighted it against her the best he could."

"I expected that," Alex calmly said. "It won't matter."

155

"If she survives the list, the last she will fight will be Phillip."

Alex nodded. "Thanks Cal."

Cal's eyes scanned my body, and smiled approvingly at Alex. I watched his smile vanish and he hurried on his way.

Alex headed for the door without a word and I followed. I couldn't believe my first match was going to be in the Arena. My stomach was doing horrible flips. New fighters were never in the Arena for their first fight, they lacked the experience that the people craved.

Alex led me to the gate. We waited silently and I was glad that he didn't glance back at me. He got me here, and I wanted to run away. The announcer said my name and I stopped breathing. Alex led me out, and I absently followed him into the Arena. The crowd seemed very mixed. I heard cheers, rude comments, booing, and laughter.

Alex stopped, and I almost ran into him. My courage had vanished again, and my hands were shaking. What was I thinking? Maybe Marty *was* on my side, and I had been too stubborn to notice.

Alex turned and stepped closer, bringing me away from my self-doubt. I glanced up at him, shaking my head.

"I can't do this Alex, there's just no way," I hastily said.

"You're the best fighter born in this land," he sincerely replied.

I shook my head as I watched my opponent step onto the field. I didn't hear his name, but he was huge. His biceps were the size of my head.

CHAPTER FOURTEEN

"Breathe," Alex whispered. It wasn't until his hand touched my face that I understood what he was saying, and breathed in deeply and out slowly. "This will be in two parts. You will fight until one of you makes two marks, and then there will be a short breather before the match will finish with someone acquiring three marks."

I nodded. I remember him explaining this to me when I was a kid. Three marks, that's all I had to do.

"Just focus, remember your training," he said. I nodded again and his hand slid way. He walked back the way we had entered, leaving me alone to fight my first match.

I stared at the big man before me. His armor had many weaknesses, but I had a feeling that very few people ever got close enough to hit them.

The object is to get the dominant position on your opponent. Or as Alex liked to say: *dead,* because in a real battle you would be dead. You weren't supposed to go for blood, but it was the Tournament and you came to win.

Lord Vertas didn't always come to the Tournament, but when he did, it was by his hand that the matches in the Arena began. I forced myself to look away from my opponent and glance around the stands until I found the shaded spot that made me even more nervous. That was where Lord Vertas sat.

Lord Vertas' family had ruled this land for four generations. It was during their rule that the idea of dragons had become stories. The stories of the malicious dragons had come to an end, making him a beloved ruler still today. It is said that Lord Vertas, although strict in his rule, was extremely humble. I suppose the fact that Alex convinced him to take mercy on my father, allowed me to accept that.

I hadn't actually ever met Lord Vertas. I had been young when he came to kill my father, and he didn't so much as look at my sister and I. I wish that thought had slipped my mind as I glanced over at the shaded area. I swallowed hard, not only was I going to be fighting my first fight in the Arena, but I was fighting in front of Lord Vertas. He wouldn't know who I was. It was a long time ago.

I began to feel sick to my stomach. What if he did, would he delight in seeing me fail? Was that why my father was so against me doing this? Was Lord Vertas hoping that I would not succeed? He was said to be a great swordsman himself, which is why the Tournament is held. Would he be disgraced if I, a swordsman from his land, failed in the first round?

I took my low guard, trying to keep my arms from shaking, which I knew had been a pathetic attempt because of the laughter. I stared at the enormous man in front of me, and from the corner of my eye, I watched for the signal.

Lord Vertas' hand slid out of the shadows, and as he lowered his hand, the match began. I blocked the big guy's first swing, which sent me to the ground. In one step he had his first mark. I stood up and immediately took my stance. He moved in right away with his attack. This time I dodged his swing, but his fist made contact with my face. I hit the ground rolling and continued to roll to move out of the way of my opponent's attack and instantly got to my feet again. Four moves later he had his second mark.

What was I doing here?! I was naïve to think that I could win the Tournament, let alone survive the first round. I stayed on the ground staring up at the blue sky until a shadow moved over me. In the next moment, Alex was pulling me to my feet.

"I am so sorry, Alex. You must be so embarrassed."

"Don't apologize to me. I'm not the one out here fighting against the mountain," he replied as he put a towel that stung on my cheek. His tone was light, and I knew he was just trying to cheer me up.

"Alex, I…"

"You just need to focus. Your mind is everywhere, but on the moment. You are a better fighter than you're showing. Forget where you are for a moment. When the match is ready to start, close your eyes, take a few seconds and center yourself. Vertas will see this, and he'll wait until you open your eyes."

"How…"

"It's what every great fighter used to do." Alex removed the towel and gently touched the other side of my face with his hand. "You can do this."

I still felt his touch lingering after he walked away. I shook my head, and focused on the *mountain* that was standing before me. I closed my eyes as I stepped into my low guard. I waited until I couldn't hear the crowd anymore before I opened my eyes. A second later, I saw Lord Vertas drop his hand.

My sword came up, and met his near his head. He pushed and I moved backwards, but I didn't fall. I swung my sword around quickly and he blocked and pushed me away, and then again. I smiled as I realized that all I had to do was change things up a bit. This time when he pushed my sword away, I turned the opposite way and moved behind him, and then… *dead.*

I waited until he took his stance, and attacked a heartbeat later. My sword clanged against his twice and then… *dead.* I focused on his eyes, and let him attack. He swung and missed. He attempted to stab his blade through me, but I moved quicker and… *dead.*

To my surprise my opponent tilted his head at me. The crowd around us became a yelling frenzy. It was so chaotic that I wasn't sure if they were excited or angry. Alex walked out to me, and wrapped his arms around me.

"I told you, you could do it!" he cheered. "You beat John! It'll be easy now until you get to Phillip in the last round."

161

I looked at him, and saw how proud he was. I couldn't contain the excitement that I felt from winning my first match, my first match in the Arena! Add to that the expression on Alex's face, and there was nothing else that mattered to me.

We walked out of the Arena to another section of the facility where the other matches were being held. It was overflowing with people.

"Hey Alex, nice piece of meat," a man yelled before we had entered the facility. "Probably will be better after it has been tenderized!"

Before I had unsheathed my sword, Alex had his blade against the man's throat. I didn't hear the words that were being exchanged, but the man paled and nearly collapsed as Alex let go of him.

I smiled at the man, but I really wanted to drive my blade into him. Alex walked toward the entrance without a glance at the man that was hurrying away, and motioned for me to enter first. The heckling didn't stop, in fact it got worse. I glared at them, knowing that they would be eating their words at the end of the day. I did not fight for my opportunity to win the Tournament to be chased away by men who didn't even know how to wield a sword.

Alex pointed out that there were four open spaces around us. There were three men and one woman, each fighting against one of Marty's boys. I quickly noticed that the open spaces were not nearly as big as the Arena.

"This is where you'll fight the rest of your matches," Alex whispered in my ear. I glimpsed over at him as a strange sensation moved through me. He met my eyes for a moment, but quickly looked away from me before he continued, "You'll have to be mindful of the small space. The spaces are to make the matches quicker. Most of these men are experienced fighters and have fought in Tournaments before. They know how to make the limited space work to their advantage.

"There will be four matches today, ten tomorrow, and when you win all of those, the next morning at sunrise you will face off with Phillip. If you win against him, then there will be one more match, but if you lose the Tournament will be over."

"Why are you so confident that Phillip is going be my last competitor?" I asked as Alex led me to my next fight.

"Because no man has ever beaten him. All of his fights will be in the Arena. He is one of the reasons that there are so many here today. Many of the swordsmen are hoping to get a chance to beat him, but most just want to catch a glimpse of what Marty's son is capable of."

I stopped, unsure of where I was going. As I turned toward Alex, he was shoved into me and his arms immediately embraced me to keep me from falling. There were suddenly too many people trying to get passed us, causing Alex to not let go of me. I glanced up at his face to see his eyes searching.

"Ahh, there it is," he said, directing my eyes with his chin.

I looked over in that direction, but I couldn't see anything but the mass of people. Alex took me by the hand and pulled me to where he wanted to go.

163

People continued to attempt to push me away from where I was trying to go and I couldn't escape the notion that it was on purpose. Luckily, Alex had a good grip on my hand and pulled me towards him before letting go of my hand.

We were standing in front of the gate to one of the Tournament fields. I glanced back at him, and he smiled down at me.

"You're not nervous again are you?"

I shook my head and he smiled, knowing that I wasn't being honest. Alex put his hand on the entrance gate and John, the man I had just defeated, stepped in front of the gate, preventing Alex from opening it. My body tensed immediately. Was he going to take his loss out on me now?!

"Alex," he said in a voice that was as deep as he was huge.

"John," Alex replied, but didn't move.

John wasn't wearing his armor anymore, and he didn't look any smaller. He had long brown hair that was pulled back tight away from his face. He smiled and seemed more like a teddy bear than he did a fearsome warrior. I couldn't help but smile back.

"I should have known I was going to lose. Alex, here, is amazing at scouting out strong spirited warriors." He looked over at me, and then at Alex. "I must say she's the prettiest you've ever found."

I looked down as the compliment made my ears burn. "John, is there something I can help you with," Alex inquired.

"I… uh, I'll be rooting for you, Sonia," he quickly said. "I think if anyone can beat Phillip at this Tournament it will be you."

"Thank you, John," I softly replied, not sure what I thought about his comment.

"Good luck," he said, bowing his head at me. I watched him glance at Alex and walk over to the small crowd that was gathering for the fight I was about to be in.

"He doesn't seem to care that he lost," I commented as we entered the gate.

"He's been in a lot of Tournaments. He only fights because Vertas asks him to."

"He's not very good?" I asked.

"No, he's quite good. Marty was hoping that John would pummel you, and you'd be out," Alex informed me.

"So, it's *not* set that I'll be fighting Phillip."

"No, you could lose at any of these matches, and that would be it. There are no second chances and no re-dos."

Was that why my first fight had been in the Arena? Marty was going to embarrass me… or worse Alex.

"That's good to be reminded of," I replied, feeling the pressure again.

"So, if you want a chance at Phillip, you need to win these."

I remembered the look in Phillip's eyes before he kissed me. My anger surged at the memory of him kissing me. I wanted a piece of Phillip. His ego needed to be knocked down.

165

Okay, so I had to win everything. The quicker I won, the sooner it would be over, and the more rest I'd get. I stepped onto the field, and glanced at my opponent. He was half the size of John, but still a good foot taller than me.

He glared at me, and when a tall thin man dropped Lord Vertas's flag, he got the first point.

"Females shouldn't be allowed to fight. This is such a waste of my time," he said as I was getting up.

I zeroed in on him, and won the match without another hit from him. I held onto the memory of Phillip, and easily won the next three matches.

Alex walked me back to our room. Everything seemed much calmer, and that was a nice change. Today had gone quite well, and Alex was very proud of me. As we stepped into our room, I saw my father waiting for me.

He immediately wrapped his arms around me. "I brought some food. Are you hungry?"

"Starving," I smiled. He had set up dinner on a table and we all walked over to it.

"Where's Krissy?" Alex asked, and I glanced over at him.

"She was invited to dine elsewhere," my father replied.

"How's your day been?" I causally asked, not wanting to hear about Krissy.

"Crazy. We're selling better than at the last Tournament," he smiled. "You should hear all the rumors out there."

"Rumors?" I inquired.

"There's been a lot of talk about you. I half think that it is the reason that we're doing so well at the market."

"What kind of rumors?"

My father's eyes flitted over at Alex and he smiled uncomfortably. I tilted my head at him, waiting for him to answer my question.

"I was able to watch your first match," he stated after a moment of silence. "And I worried the rest of the day until you got here."

"Father," I smiled. It was nice to hear his concern and relief, and I allowed the subject to change.

"She's been quite amazing," Alex stated. "You watched her most difficult match."

"I thought that huge man was going to kill her in the beginning. But wow, did you ever look incredible out there!"

"Thanks," I said in astonishment.

"Have you had any trouble? Any sore losers?" Father asked. It wasn't an unwarranted concern to be worried about. There tended to be more bloodshed after a match than during one.

"Not really. I think that having Alex with me deters anyone from even thinking about trying anything."

"Don't sell yourself short," my father smiled. "A lot of men seem to be intimidated by you as well."

I couldn't believe how proud my father was. He didn't even want me in this Tournament, and yet, he was here telling me how great I was. My day could not get any better. I glanced over at Alex, knowing that he was the reason I was here.

I listened to him and my father talk about the fight, the crowds, the mishmash of people that were here, and all the things that people were saying. Everything was peaceful, and the day's excitement began to take its toll.

"I should get going so that you can get some sleep," my father stated.

"You don't have to go," I told him.

"Krissy and I have a room near the market. Alex will keep you safe, and I'll watch over Krissy."

I stood up as my father did, and walked with him to the door. "I won't make it to your first match tomorrow, but I will try to see at least one, so don't lose until after I do," he smiled, and I stared at him in surprise. "You were amazing," he whispered as he hugged me.

I watched him turn and walk away. I glanced back at Alex. It felt odd that we were going to be sleeping in the same room, but this was how the Tournament was set up - a designated space for trainer and swordsman.

"How are you feeling?" Alex asked.

"For the first time today, I feel tired."

Alex chuckled, and walked over to me. "Well, let's get you out of this armor so you can sleep."

He undid all the fasteners and slid the armor over my head. "Thank you," I said. "For all your... help."

He didn't reply, and I glanced up at his face. He looked shocked, but as my eyes met his, I didn't care what surprised him. His disbelief melted into affection, and he tucked my hair behind my ear.

"It's been my pleasure," he softly said. His face was moving closer and I didn't know what to think, but I wasn't moving away.

"You should get some sleep," he quietly remarked, and I nodded, but neither of us stepped away. His face had moved within inches of mine. His breath caressed my lips, and my mind relaxed even more.

"Tomorrow is going to be a long day," he stated as his eyes shifted away from me.

I took a step back, and stared at the floor. I didn't understand what was going on, and suddenly I feared that he was going to leave.

"Will you practice with me in the morning?" I quickly asked, but I didn't look at him.

"Yes," he replied.

Of course he wasn't going to leave, the Tournament was all day tomorrow. I turned and walked over to the bed, finding it strange that I had worried that he was going to leave. I had just laid my head down, when I heard him close the door. He walked over to me and a blanket covered me. He whispered strange, but beautiful words, and a moment later my eyes closed as sleep washed over me.

CHAPTER FIFTEEN

I abruptly sat up, barely awake. My pulse was quicker than it should be, but I had no idea what I had been dreaming about. Whatever it had been, it had left fear lingering in my mind.

"Alex," I said slightly louder than a whisper. To my surprise there was no answer. I cautiously got out of bed. "Alex?"

I walked over to the other bed which was near the alcove that Storm was in. He wasn't there, and neither was Storm. Panic began to move through me. No, he told me he'd be here in the morning. Maybe he took Storm out to run. I didn't imagine that a big horse like Storm enjoyed being cramped up in such a small space.

I was wide awake now, and decided that I would go see if they were outside. I opened the door, and a cool breeze blew in. I glanced down the hallway to see the door was open. Why was the door left open?

I shivered as I stepped out of the room, heading towards the open door. I exited the building and was startled by how dark it was. What was I doing? It must be the middle of the night. I was about to turn and go back in, but I halted as I heard a horse neighing.

I scanned the vicinity, but I didn't see anyone. An ominous feeling was moving through me as I walked in the direction I had heard the horse, causing me to wish I had grabbed my sword.

A sense of dread was building inside of me with each step I took. I was halfway to the meadow outside of the Arena when I decided that I didn't want to check up on Alex. I knew seeing Alex would make me feel better, but I didn't even know if he was out here.

I hurried back the way I came when I heard a man talking. It sounded like the man that had shown Alex my schedule...Cal. Was he talking with Alex? I walked into a grove of trees, and cautiously moved towards the voice. As I saw that whoever Cal was talking to wasn't Alex, I quickly hid behind a tree. I peeked back around to see Cal talking to a large man in a cloak.

"You're sure," the large man said. "Because they do not like it when things don't go their way."

"Yes, I know," Cal said as he rubbed his bandaged arm.

What happened to him? His arm wasn't bandaged earlier.

"She is better than we had expected," Cal stated. "But Marty has got everything under control."

"Ha!" the other man said loudly. "If anyone is in control it is Alex, and we both have seen how distracted he's become."

"I did notice. He's usually checking out all the...talent."

171

"His kind are not to be trifled with, so don't go near the girl."

"I'm not stupid. She is focused and…"

"*Spirited*."

"Umm…yes," Cal said cautiously.

"My mistress is most curious about her," the other man remarked.

"Well, she…"

Cal stopped talking as the other man's head came up. He looked around and I ducked back behind the tree, hoping that he didn't see me. I didn't understand this conversation at all. What talent was Alex usually searching for? I never noticed him looking at anyone? John did say he was a good scout… And what was Alex's *kind*?

"Don't worry he is talking with Lord Vertas right now," Cal said, and I peeked back around the tree again. I knew I should head back to my room, but I wanted to know what was going on.

"Are you sure? Because this night could go very badly if he isn't."

"Lord Vertas sent for him," Cal informed the other man. "I delivered the message myself."

"Really? Hmm… Perhaps they can straighten things out and we'll be back on track."

"The girl cannot…"

There was a noise to the left of them, and Cal nervously turned his head.

"Ortal," the large man said after a moment with disgust and a tinge of fear,.

"Ortal?" Cal echoed.

I forced myself to swallow. The Ortal were *here*? How come that man was not as afraid as he should have been? It didn't matter. If the Ortal were out here, then I needed to get back to my sword.

"Don't worry they're not searching for you. Plus, the Alpha would not do anything with Lord Vertas so close."

"You don't sound very confident," Cal pointed out.

"They have a job that doesn't include us. However sometimes they get sidetracked. Perhaps you should return to your room before they become... distracted," the man growled, and I was certain he was threatening Cal.

I quietly moved away and walked quickly back to my room. I was half way back when I saw a large man standing between me and the entrance. It looked like the same cloaked man that was talking with Cal, but it couldn't be. The ominous feeling that had been growing earlier surged forward, pulling my fears along with it.

I knew that I did not want to go near that man. I hastily turned down a nearby alley, deciding that I would go to the other entrance. I turned down the next road that would lead me passed the markets and to the entrance I wanted to get to. There were very few people out, and I wasn't sure if that was a good thing or a bad thing.

I took a deep breath, trying to calm the desire to sprint down the road. I was sure that I did not want to bring any attention to myself. The Ortal were around, and the man that Cal had been talking with added more anxiety to my thoughts. I needed to get back to my room.

As I turned the next corner, I saw Alex. Relief washed over me until I saw a woman step close to him. She had long, golden hair, and there was no Lord Vertas anywhere to be seen. He had a drink in one hand and was laughing.

I shook my head, what did it matter. He was Alex, he should be out having a good time. It's not like he was fighting tomorrow. The woman suddenly glanced in my direction and I squished myself against the building I was next to.

What was wrong with me? It's not like she knew who I was. I tried to get myself to relax. I was being ridiculous.

I glimpsed back to see not Alex, but a man with dark hair smiling stupidly at the woman. He abruptly turned towards me with a serious expression and began to move in my direction. As the roar of the Shadow Dragon filled the night, the man quickly disappeared into the shadows. My eyes shifted to the beautiful woman with long, golden hair who was staring at me.

She appeared delicate and harmless, and yet there was sense of warning moving through me. I instantly thought of how Phillip's handsome looks made me uneasy too. I turned to go back the way I came, but the large man in the cloak was standing in the alley as though he was waiting for me to run that way.

I was being paranoid. How would he know that I would double back? As the question entered my mind, I began to wonder if this had all been set up. The man's words echoed in my mind, *Because this night could go very badly if he isn't.*

It was just all the pressure from the day. I'm sure that I was just over-reacting. Cal and that man never said my name, they could have been talking about anyone.

"Kind of late for you to be out, isn't it little girl?" a man inquired rhetorically as I turned to walk in another direction.

"The Ortal have spoken of your strength," the woman said in a strange voice. "Sonia, is it?"

I turned to glance over at her again, she was only a few feet away from me. Her voice was friendly, but my mind was yelling that I should be running. How was it even possible that she understood the Ortal? She must have heard the rumors of my survival... My rationalizing was not soothing my unease. I turned away from her and took a step towards the other side of the road.

"I don't think you'll be leaving just yet," she sweetly said, and I glanced back at her. "I'd like to get to know the girl that is getting so much attention."

I shook my head, and she stared at me curiously. I glanced back at the large man again, who had moved into the street that the lady and I were standing in. He had lowered the hood of his cloak, and I saw the three eyes and ugly green skin.

I began to run as it clicked that he was the same creature that had attacked me with an axe. I heard his heavy footsteps behind me, luckily he sounded slower than me. I glanced over my shoulder to see that he was still a good distance behind me and that brought a little relief to my mind. However, as I turned my head the woman was in front of me.

I halted and turned to run down another street.

"Stop," the woman said, and my body listened to her. "Staltam, would you mind helping me?" she asked with a smile.

"Of course not, my Mistress," he replied as he caught up with me. I wanted to run, but I couldn't get one foot in front of the other. Why wasn't I running?!

"We need to leave here. Quickly, before someone notices her. Let's take her to the grove." The woman's eyes focused on me and she smiled innocently. "Let's go for a walk, and no screaming."

Again my body obeyed her words. Staltam wrapped his huge hand around my arm and walked me to a grove of thick trees behind the facility that I was supposed to be sleeping in. I was trying to struggle to run away from them, but my body wasn't listening to me.

"So, you are the girl that Phillip is so fascinated with? I see nothing special about you."

"That's because you're not looking right," Marty said as he stepped from the trees in front of me.

I was surprised, angry, and afraid. Why was he so against me?!

"You have to look passed her mortality, to see what Aleksertac sees."

WHO?!

The woman eyed him suspiciously, before she walked over to him.

"Was she any trouble?" Marty asked.

"Unfortunately, no. With all the rumors that are flying about her I expected to have some fun," she pouted as she stepped very close to him.

"Don't worry, you'll have your fun," he stated as he stared at me.

That did not sound good, and the malice in his eyes only reinforced my fears. The woman laughed with anticipation.

I had to get out of here.

The woman placed her hand on Marty's shoulder, moving her body close to his side. Marty's hand slid to the small of her back as he smiled at me. He slowly turned his head and lowered his face to hers. She stood on her toes and kissed him.

At that moment, my legs worked. Staltam's grip on me was totally lax and I was free of his grip. Without any hesitation I sprinted away from them. I heard Marty's frustrated yell, and I pushed myself faster.

Two men in cloaks appeared as I exited the grove. I dodged the first one, but the second one caught me, and threw me to the ground. I was up in an instant, but before I was able to run again the woman was standing before me.

"Stay," she said with a smile, but her eyes showed her frustration.

"Staltam, do you think you can keep a hold of her this time?"

"Of course, Madam."

The woman was moving closer to me, holding a dagger up as though she were going to stab it into me. There were three cloaked creatures besides Staltam, and I shook my head in denial that any of this was actually happening. Staltam grabbed a fist full of my hair, and yanked my head back so that I was staring at the stars above. I desperately searched the sky for the Shadow's orbs of fire. I had heard him. Where was he? I glanced at the woman as she ran her fingers down my neck before tightly gripping my shoulder. She was smiling with anticipation.

"We just need your..."

Storm reared in front me, neighing angrily. The woman fell to the ground with a startled scream, and Staltam released me. She hissed at Storm, and his front feet came to the ground with thunder. Had the woman not moved, Storm's hooves would have gone through her. I looked up as Alex grabbed me, pulling me onto the horse. A moment later Storm was racing away from the grove.

"What were you doing?!" Alex stated, clearly annoyed. "During the Tournament, people should... *you* shouldn't have left the room."

"Where were you?!" I growled, not liking how he was talking to me.

"I had a meeting with Vertas."

"Oh, so you can leave, but I have to stay?" I inquired curtly. "I..."

"I'm not being hunted by Ortal," he growled as we arrived at the building. "And *I* didn't leave my sword in the room?"

With all that had just happened I had forgotten about the Ortal. They had a job, the cloaked man had said. Their job was to hunt *me*?! Alex slid off of Storm and began to lead him to our room without a glance back at me.

"They're *hunting* me?" I said to his back, trying to hide the fear that I felt. He paused for a moment and his shoulders slumped.

I should have been angry at him for talking to me like he was, but the mention of the Ortal took all my irritation away. He had every right to talk to me like a child. I had acted like one. I had walked out into the night as though the Ortal hadn't already made two attempts to capture, or kill, me.

"Why?" I inquired in a whisper. Why was every...thing so interested in me?

Alex turned back around, all his anger was gone. He reached up to me and I slid into his arms, but I quickly moved away from him.

"I shouldn't have left you. Vertas sent for me after you fell asleep. I didn't think I'd be gone long."

I walked passed him into our room as he opened the door, feeling confused. Alex followed behind me, not saying another word. As he closed the door, I stopped walking. I slid my hand into my hair, debating what I wanted to tell Alex.

"I overheard Cal talking to that three eyed man... thing," I began despondently. "They were talking about..."

I stopped talking when I couldn't remember. I thought about the woman with the golden hair... Who was she? Why... *how* did my body obey her?

179

She was going to use her dagger to… for what and why?

I shook my head, and stared at Alex who was standing in front of me now, his eyes full of empathy.

"Are you alright?" he asked, moving his hand toward my face.

"I'm just tired," I lied.

I didn't know what to talk to him about, and I wasn't sure how I felt about all that had happened tonight. Alex touched my face, but I didn't look at him. I moved away, thinking about all the awful things that had happened to me in the last few months. All I wanted to do was be in the Tournament and win. Why was everything against me?

I laid back down on my bed, and stared at the wall. Alex laid a blanket over me, and after a few moments he walked away. I took a deep breath and tried to clear my mind. I began focusing on the Tournament.

I was going to win. Everything was against me, which meant that I *had* to win. There was no room for error tomorrow. I was going to win to show the world that I would not be bullied or chased away from what I wanted. The world would know that I was not to be trifled with.

I closed my eyes, repeating to myself the importance of winning tomorrow. There was no other option.

CHAPTER SIXTEEN

I was not in the first match, but Alex had me watching a fight that involved an opponent that he was impressed with.

"See how he coaxes in his opponent. He's been watching you, and I think he's anticipating the challenge. He's been fighting a long time, but your style isn't what he's used to," Alex informed me as we watched, and I nodded that I understood.

I awoke irritable this morning, but very focused on what I needed to accomplish. I could barely remember the events of the other night. Had this been the first surreal thing to have happened to me, I would have believed I had dreamt the beautiful woman and Marty.

I clenched my jaw, just the thought of Marty reminded me why I was going to win this.

"Just don't move into his traps," Alex stated, bringing my mind back into focus. He is an experienced swordsman and hunter. Watch... There did you see that?"

"Yes," I answered, feeling my nerves tighten in my stomach. He was really good at maneuvering people to get his point.

"You're better than him. Don't for...get that."

I glanced over at Alex as his voice faded away. He was staring at the end of the bleachers, but I didn't see anything.

"Alex?"

"Will you excuse me?" he asked kindly, but he seemed distracted.

"Of course," I replied, not understanding what had grabbed his attention.

I watched him disappear into the crowd before I focused back at the fight in front of me. This guy was battling one of Marty's boys, Paul - one of the better boys. The guy only needed one more mark, but at the moment he wasn't even trying. As much fun as it was to watch him infuriate Paul, a part of me was irritated by the man's overconfidence. I'd have finished it already.

"He's pretty impressive, isn't he?" a voice that I didn't recognize said.

I didn't respond to him. No one here was important to me, only the competition. I needed to absorb as much about this guy as I could. I wanted to be able to bring him down as quick as I...

"You are the last female in the Tournament. I can make sure you reach the top," he continued, and slid his hand onto my leg. I glared at him and moved away. He smiled happily. "You can't expect to make it on your own. Marty told me *all* about you."

I stood up, and walked away. Of course I could win this on my own. Who did that guy think he was? I scanned the crowd for Alex, but didn't see him. I stood by the tall wooden fence, and continued watching the match.

I could see what Alex was talking about, and understood why he made sure that I watched this man. He reminded me of a predator playing with his prey. I found myself pulling for Paul, but not because I didn't want to go against this guy. I actually was certain that I would triumph over him, but he reminded me of Phillip and I wanted him to lose.

My anger was growing in me again. From Phillip, my thoughts fell to him and Alex talking, him kissing me, Marty trying to personally take me out of the Tournament, all the cat-calls, the looks of disgust that I would even try to be here. And now, Alex left me without any explanation, and that guy had the nerve to think that I would allow him to touch me. Not to mention that Alex has been talking with Marty, Lord Vertas, and who knew who else. Phillip was the expected winner and I was supposed to have lost already.

If anyone is in control it is Alex. What could that possibly mean?! Was Alex...

A body pushed hard against mine, "We can be nice about this, or we can..."

I jammed my elbow into his gut, unsheathed my sword, and turned. "Touch me again, and you won't live another day," I growled, holding my sword at his neck. His eyes lit up with fear, and I pushed him away from me. I was not a prize, or some helpless, insignificant female!

Instead of turning to leave, the man glared at me, and pulled out a short sword. "Come on, little girl, let's see what you can do."

183

"Excuse me, Tom, is there a problem here?" Alex asked, stepping in between us.

"Alex… What? No. No problem. I was just…"

"Leaving?" Alex inquired, his dark eyes not the least bit friendly.

"Yea. Leaving. I was… Nice to see you again," the man stuttered before quickly disappearing.

"Are you alright?" Alex inquired as he turned his attention to me.

"Nothing I couldn't handle," I replied with irritation.

"If you had fought him, you would have been penalized in your standing in the Tournament."

"What? I should have just let him do whatever he wanted?!"

"No, I won't…"

"*I* won't be chased away from this, Alex!" I growled. "No one, is going to stop me. No one."

"I know," he softly said, and I suddenly felt bad for growling at him. I was about to apologize, but his gaze moved passed me and his jaw tightened and relaxed before his eyes shifted back to me. "Are you ready," he asked distantly.

"Yes," I curtly stated.

I was annoyed at the whole situation that had just unfolded. Did the other females in this Tournament submit to Tom? Or did they fight back and that was why I was the last female in the Tournament? That thought strengthened my anger. We all *earned* our right to be here. I had better not see that guy again, or he would bleed.

Alex and I walked to the gate in silence. He did not enter with me this time, but I was too annoyed to care. I unsheathed my sword, waiting for my opponent. I deserved to be here. If the other women took his offer, then they shouldn't have come. I trained and I...I didn't even want to think about all the injuries I had acquired, or all the creatures that shouldn't exist.

I focused in front of me as my opponent stepped to the center. I became furious as I saw the man who referred to me as meat yesterday standing before me. I tightened my grip on my sword, and took my low guard. He was going down.

He sneered as the sign to begin was given. I didn't hesitate, I drove my blade at him, barely missing my point. He got an easy point out of my hastiness, and I clenched my jaw. I didn't even glance at Alex, whom I knew was disappointed. I took my stance, and waited for him to move.

As soon as he shifted, I moved my sword up and turned all the way around. When my sword came down, it fell with such strength that the man collapsed to his knees, dropping his sword. I kicked the man to the ground, and held the tip of my blade at his neck. *Dead.*

I focused on the man, but did not move right away.

"I cannot wait to get you on your back," he hissed.

We were moved back to our stance, and had to wait for the signal again before we began because I

185

hadn't moved away from him quick enough. It took everything I had to not drive my blade through him.

The hand of the man holding the flag started to shake, and I tightened the hold on my sword again. I thought about how Phillip seemed to believe that all I was good for was a prize to be won. This man thought that I was a piece of meat...

The flag dropped, I moved instantly, and swung. The man blocked, and I kicked him away. He rolled away from me, and quickly got to his feet.

"You must be worth it, if Alex is willing to pick up Marty's seconds."

I yelled my anger as I swung harder until I had *him* on his back with his fear sweating off his face.

"Dead," I whispered, through my teeth.

I had two points, and I went to a section of the wooden fence where there was no one. I didn't check to see where Alex was, I couldn't decide if I needed to calm down, or hold onto this anger.

"You look good out there."

I glanced up to see Phillip standing on the other side of the fence. Where did he come from?

"You have this win easy. I anticipating finishing our little competition," he slyly said and shifted his attention passed me.

I turned to see where he was focused, and saw Alex talking with Marty *again*. I don't know why it irked me, but it did. It was probably because I was stuck here speaking with the one person I despised almost as much as Marty. Alex glanced my way, but quickly looked back at Marty. He made no attempt to excuse himself from Marty, to get Phillip away from me, and this just fed my anger.

"Sonia," Phillip called, and I glanced over at him. He smiled charmingly at me, "Good Luck."

I glared at him and turned quickly, staring at my opponent with loathing. This day needed to end! I stormed to the center, and precariously took my stance. The man smiled as though he thought I was going to let him win. I don't think so.

As the flag fell, I tightened my arms, focusing in on the man in front of me. I allowed him to make the first move, and in four moves I had won.

I walked out of the enclosed area, and saw a woman speaking with Alex and Marty, but her eyes were fixed on Alex. Grr... I didn't even pause, I continued to my next match.

I watched Henry, another one of Marty's boys, step onto the field with a smug smile. I could feel my anger beginning to rage. This match was over before it started. I walked off the field without a second glance at Henry who was flat on his back. Alex continued to conveniently be held up by someone else instead of with me, which only fed my irritation.

The next match Alex came over to me at the break to fix my armor that had come loose. His eyes never once came to my face, and he didn't say one word. What was going on? He was never like this to me. He always told me what I needed to work on, and what he was glad to see that I was doing. Today, he seemed somewhere else.

187

Why did it even matter?! I came here to win a Tournament. He evidently had only planned to get me through the first day, and then let me fend for myself. Oh yea, he was scouting out the talent.

Whatever.

I finished this match, and continued winning the next four matches. As I stepped onto the field for my last match, I saw the man that Alex had me watch first thing this morning - the experienced swordsman and hunter. I couldn't wait for this match to start. I stood in the center waiting impatiently for him to join me.

"You must either be very good, or very lucky," he stated as he stood in front of me.

"Guess you'll get to decide that for yourself."

He smiled, and took a high stance. I took my low guard, never taking my eyes off of his sword. This match lasted longer than I had wanted, but in the end, he was *dead*.

The man walked off, furious that I had won. He couldn't understand how I had out maneuvered him, even with blood gushing down my face.

Alex helped me out of my armor, and seemed to be relieved that, even though I was bleeding, I would have lots of time to rest. That last competitor slammed his fist into my face, splitting my cheek open. Unfortunately for him, this only fueled my anger and he almost ended up dead, for real.

Alex had me sit on a stool, and then pulled one up for himself. He tilted my face bloody side up. After he inspected the wound, he put a wet cloth on my cheek that had a bitter smell and stared across the room.

"I can't believe you almost killed him," Alex said, looking for something to talk about. He didn't sound like he was truly interested in the reason for it, nor did he sound like he was angry with me.

"I need to fight Phillip," I irritably said. "I need to fight him and win."

"Of course you do," he replied, lacking his usual gusto.

He wasn't making eye contact as he talked to me. Even after he removed the cloth, folded it over and replaced it again, his eyes never met mine.

I stared at him. What had I done wrong? Alex felt very distant from me. He was right next to me, but he might as well not be. I glanced around the room, thinking through everything I had done today. I won every match. He wasn't even around between the matches. I thought back to the night before. He had saved me and I went to bed. What...

He lifted the now warm and bloody cloth off of my cheek. "It's not too bad," he informed me.

"Alex, what's wrong?" I asked, as I grabbed his hand and stared at his face.

"Nothing," he lied, pulling his hand away from mine – avoiding eye contact. Alex either told me the truth or he didn't say anything.

I felt the anger burning ferociously in me. "You're lying to me!" I growled and stood up. He remained focused elsewhere. "You've **never** lied to me! I've worked so hard to get here! I shouldn't even be here, I should be dead.

189

"You spent all this time training me, healing me, and now that I'm doing everything you've always believed I could, you won't even look at me?!"

"You have one more competition. You should get some rest," he said flatly, *still* not looking at me.

"No!" I practically yelled.

I wanted to say more, but I couldn't figure out what needed to be said. I stared at the side of his face, wanting his eyes to shift to mine. If for no other reason than to show me he was proud of me, but he didn't.

I turned away from him, glimpsing around the room, taking in the bloody armor that he brought for me, the sword that he had taken me to get, the room that we were in because he healed me and trained me. Tears swelled in my eyes as I glanced back at him, feeling totally lost. He was staring down at the cloth that was soaked in my blood.

My tears were swallowed into a new surge of animosity. If it didn't matter to him, then... then he didn't matter to me. I stood up, and stormed away from him. The fact that he didn't stop me only infuriated me more. Why it did, I had no idea.

I didn't stop walking until I was out in the Arena. I stepped up to the fence to see that there was no competition going on here either. The bleachers were mostly empty. I thought that there were supposed to be matches in this arena until dusk. This just added to my irritation. I needed something to focus on! I needed a distraction, anything other than this horrible feeling that was coursing through my body.

I slammed my fists on the fence, and stared at the empty Arena. I had all this energy, and no outlet for it. Why did Alex seem so far away from me? He never made me feel this way. He was always excited about everything I did, and now that I have something that he should actually be excited for, he wasn't the least bit interested.

I guess he *was* like all the other guys, disliking a woman for being anything but at home. That theory made no sense, since it was because of him that I *was* here and I knew it. Unless... unless he never believed that I would actually make it this far. My knees almost buckled with that thought. Could one person be that cruel?

"Sonia," Alex called to me.

I didn't look, or acknowledge that I heard him. I just focused on the field that I was going to have my final match on, the field that I was going to take Marty's son down in front of everyone.

"Sonia," Alex whispered from right behind me. I felt butterflies in my stomach, but I ignored them. I was too angry. The mere thought that he was expecting me to fail, made me want to fight him.

He stepped next to me, and when I didn't acknowledge him, he put his fingers under my chin to turn my face towards his. "I am very proud of you," he said with affection.

"Whatever," I said, fighting the urge to argue with him.

"I..."

"I don't want to hear it!" I growled, and jerked my face away from his touch. At the moment I

191

didn't want to hear anything he had to say. I wanted to get far from him, but for some unknown reason I couldn't get myself to move away.

"Sonia…" he started softly. His fingers tucked my hair behind my ear, and tears filled my eyes.

"Alex," John's deep voice interrupted, and Alex's hand fell to his side.

I didn't turn to glance at John. I continued to stare at the Arena floor, hoping that Alex would leave to go speak with John.

"What's wrong, John?" Alex curiously asked.

"Lord Vertas has decided that Phillip and Sonia will fight this evening."

"What?! She needs to rest," he argued.

No, I didn't.

"I know, but it's been agreed that since the competition ended so early, and Phillip has assured Lord Vertas that he is ready to fight Sonia…"

"When is it supposed to begin?" he inquired, and I knew he was forcing himself to stay calm.

Isn't this what he wanted?

"In fifteen minutes," John cautiously replied.

"Let's get it over with then," I said angrily before Alex could argue. I walked away from them, not paying attention to either of them.

"Thank you for the information," Alex said, and then hurried to catch up to me.

Alex remained silent as we walked back to the room, but I didn't care. I was reeling in the chaos of emotions that I felt at the moment.

"I should have known that Marty would speed this up," Alex grumbled as he picked my armor up off the ground.

"Maybe he and Krissy should hook up," I curtly said to myself, or so I had thought.

"What does that mean?" Alex inquired.

"She's been bitter about this Tournament ever since you said that you'd train me. She's even been speaking with Phillip…" I stopped mid-sentence as I remembered the way that Phillip verbally recalled who Krissy was. And I remember overhearing Percy say how charming Phillip was.

"Sonia?" he asked as he finished fastening my armor.

I felt my anger rising into ferocity. "Phillip was trying to ooze his way into my good graces before my first match. He had made it sound like he had more than just *met* my sister…" I blurted out as the pieces began falling together. And you…"

I glared up at him. That's when I saw that Alex had walked me out into the Arena, and I hadn't even noticed, but for the moment I didn't care. I watched Alex glare at Phillip before he turned to leave, turned to leave before I was done talking with him. I scowled at his back, and then turned my anger towards Phillip who was smiling haughtily at Alex's back.

It hit me all at once. Before the Tournament started, Phillip had seen Alex coming… that's what Phillip had meant by *let the competition begin*. Was that why Alex was so far away from me? Phillip wasn't talking about his competition with me, but *for* me. I watched as Phillip looked around the Arena, smiling with all his *charm* to the crowd. His eyes met mine and I became enraged.

"I'm ready to end this competition, how about you?" Phillip stepped closer to me with a devious smile.

He raised his sword, and I focused on him with all my rage. I saw Lord Vertas drop his hand, and I attacked without missing a beat. Our swords collided, and I saw Phillip's surprise turn into entertainment. He attacked, forcing me off my offense so that I had to block. I wanted the first point. I wanted him to compete against me, not Alex.

He hesitated his next attack, and I took advantage of that. I came at him hard, and after four hits I moved myself around him, forcing him to turn quickly. His stance was not solid and I swept his legs out from underneath him. The first mark was mine. The astonishment on his face was satisfying as I watched him get up.

"Don't underestimate her," Marty yelled.

I thought about all the awful things his father had done to me, and I focused harder. When Phillip started his attack, I dodged his blade, moving so that he had to turn, and I became the attacker. We used the entire floor of the Arena, taking turns attacking and blocking. He got his first mark and I became angrier. He was *not* going to win this.

I got up, and moved quickly, not taking a stance. I could tell he was annoyed at how long this was taking, which motivated me more. He thought that I was weak, that he was going to come in here, and get all his marks right away.

"I'm going to win this," he said like a snake as he pushed his sword against mine. I shoved him away, and immediately moved into an attack.

I had him on the retreat and, by the expression on his face, I knew the strength behind my hits surprised him. He fell to the ground and bounced back up. He took a cheap shot, and I screamed at the unexpected pain as his blade sliced through my armor on my outer thigh. He came up behind me, pulling me tight against him with his blade at my neck, getting his mark.

"He has secrets," Phillip whispered in my ear. "You can't deny me what I want, and he knows it. You *will* be mine."

"I'm no one's," I forced out, trying not to show my pain.

"You have much to learn," he replied into my ear. He breathed in deep before he released me, and I collapsed to the ground against my will.

I was forcing myself up as Alex came to my side, allowing himself to be my strength to get off the field.

"Vertas has given us an extended break, so that I may attempt to fix your wound," Alex informed me.

"Why would Lord Vertas do that?" I angrily said. "His precious Phillip is winning."

"Because you have captivated his attention," Alex replied, sitting me on a bench.

His hands moved quickly to unfasten the armor. His face showed that he did not like the appearance

195

of my wound, and I decided against looking for myself.

"This isn't good, Sonia."

"Just fix it," I stated.

"Sonia…"

"If I don't get back out there then he wins! What was the point of me coming here, winning all those matches, if I don't win the one that counts!"

He nodded at me, and I saw him pull out a small jar. He filled his fingers with a gel like substance from the container I had not seen before, and shoved it into my wound. I screamed as it seared into my flesh. He quickly wrapped my thigh up before he glanced up at me, but I focused on the Arena.

"Sonia, I…"

"It's obvious that I don't know what is really going on," I began before I stared into his eyes. "But I am not a prize to be won," I growled at him, and stood up as he finished fastening the broken armor back up.

I didn't glimpse back at him to see his reaction. I hobbled out into the center of the Arena. The crowd was instantly cheering and booing, and it sounded weighted in my favor. I stepped in front of Phillip who was still smiling. I needed two marks to win and he needed one.

I closed my eyes until there was no one in the Arena, except me. I opened my eyes, saw Lord Vertas' hand drop, and attacked with such fury that I had my mark within seconds. I could hear Marty yelling in the background, but I didn't care what he was saying, he was insignificant.

Our swords came up together, and I twisted out of his way, almost getting my third mark. Phillip growled at me, but I could see the exhilaration in his eyes. His swings came harder as we continued on. Nothing existed outside of my anger and Phillip.

His sword cut across my side, but I didn't hesitate. I turned quickly, and blocked his killing strike. He laid into his sword and I almost collapsed, but I continued to fight against him and the burning in my leg, refusing to fall. I finally tilted my sword and rolled away from him.

I glanced down to see blood seeping through the pale broken armor. I glared up at Phillip, and thought about how every time I saw him, something awful happened. I hastily attacked him, which he hadn't expected, and again I almost got my mark.

Our swords collided again and again. I could feel my exhaustion, trying to win out over my will to win, and I knew that Phillip noticed. He smiled before he dove at me with a barrage of swings until I could barely stand. He hit my wrist with the hilt of his blade and my sword hit the ground. He seized me in his arms.

"See, I told you *I* would win," he whispered and rubbed his cheek against mine. "I was surprised to see you re-enter the Arena, but I can't say that I am disappointed," he whispered in my ear, his hand sliding on to my butt.

I pushed him away, and swung at him with my right hand. I hit him so hard that his face turned, and when he looked at me, blood was dripping down his face. He quickly moved and pulled me tight in his arms. His hand wrapped around the back of my neck, forcing my face closer to his.

"I do love your spirit," he smiled maliciously, "and it will be mine." He moved his face by my neck and his lips slid down to my shoulder before he released me. I collapsed to the ground and he stood over me, staring down at me with excitement. I turned my head away from him and closed my eyes.

I had lost. I had…lost. Tears stung my eyes as I laid there, not wanting to know what happened now. All that I had gone through to get here, every ounce of energy I had poured into my swordsmanship, all the awful things that I had ignored… and my father. I had done all of this against his will and failed.

CHAPTER SEVENTEEN

I felt so weak all of a sudden. The wound in my side must have been worse than I thought, but it didn't matter. Nothing did. Gentle arms scooped me off the ground, and I knew it was Alex cradling my body to his. His arms held me securely to his chest, and I found myself not wanting to be anywhere else. I opened my eyes to see he wasn't looking at me and his face expressing he wasn't happy.

"I'm sorry that I lost," I said, staring at his scowl a moment longer before closing my eyes again. I was too tired to be angry anymore. Instead, I felt overwhelmingly horrible for disappointing Alex.

"You won enough," he said just loud enough for me to hear as he sat me down, leaning my back against a cold, hard object.

I shook my head. "All of your time I wasted. You shouldn't have come back."

"You were amazing out there."

He quickly undid my armor where Phillip's sword had penetrated. A moment later the same sensation that was in my leg, burned into my side and I cried out at the pain. The tears that I had been holding back now flooded my face. Alex quickly taped and bandaged up my wound, and I tried to hold back how much I hurt, but I knew I was failing miserably.

"It's going to be okay," Alex whispered, and his fingers gently slid onto the side of my face.

I shook my head. Nothing was okay.

"You have proved to everyone you are the best."

"I lost."

"To Phillip, no man has ever beat him, not even come close, but you did."

I opened my eyes to see Alex's face close to mine.

"You have the spirit to one day be better than him," he confidently said.

This time I gazed into his eyes, I shouldn't have wanted him this close, but he made the horrible world disappear. He always found a way to make everything better. He wiped my tears from my cheek and as he moved his face closer to mine, I closed my eyes.

"Sonia," he whispered, and I felt his breath on my ear, his cheek next to mine, causing the butterflies in my stomach again. "I…"

"Alex, she has to be awarded," a deep voice yelled, bringing with it the chaos that was ensuing all around.

It was strange that up until this moment I had forgotten about the overcrowded Arena. Alex let out a sigh of frustration, and his hand slid away from me. He scooped me back up, and I opened my eyes.

He carried me through the crowd that was overwhelmingly excited for me. Was I the only one upset that I lost? Alex carried me over to some steps and stopped. I glanced up the stairs to see that they went up to Lord Vertas' shaded seat.

I immediately shifted my eyes to Alex, but he was staring at where Lord Vertas sat. His face was calm, but his eyes were making me uneasy, and I glimpsed back up the stairs. All I could see was the shadows.

"Alex, he's waiting," the deep voice said impatiently, and I looked back at Alex.

Alex set my feet down, but still held me close to him. He continued to stare up at Lord Vertas' seat, and after a moment he nodded. Alex gazed down at me, his eyes searching mine, causing my stomach to tighten up as a bad feeling rushed through me.

"You're supposed to accept your prize from Vertas. You've earned it."

"I lost," I reminded him as I stared at his chest. Alex lowered his lips to my ear, and my fingers tightened on his shirt.

"You defeated every man in this Tournament. I don't think anyone will ever say you lost. You made me proud out there."

His lips brushed my ear, and I glanced up to see him glaring towards Lord Vertas's seat. I followed his stare, realizing that Phillip was there waiting also. That was the last place I wanted to be. I looked back at Alex and slightly shook my head, but he was focused on the stairs behind me.

"Can you climb the steps?" Alex asked, sounding worried that I couldn't. However, that was probably my imagination because he didn't seem like he cared.

201

"I think so," I replied, glancing back at the steps.

Alex reluctantly let go of me, and my hands slowly released his shirt as I turned away from him. I didn't want to leave him, but I was supposed to meet Lord Vertas alone.

As I took the first step, I heard cheering. With each step, the crowd's cheering gained intensity. They were cheering as though I had won. I should have held my head high, enjoying this moment, but instead I just wanted to get away. I slowly walked up the stairs, trying to ignore the searing pain, not wanting to look up. I continued to focus on the next step until I heard the crowd become silent.

I hesitantly glanced up, and saw that Lord Vertas had actually started down the stairs. He was not an old man like I had expected, but a man around Alex's age. He moved with a regal presence that actually calmed the panic that had initially flooded my mind at the sight of him moving towards me. When he was a few stairs above me he stopped and extended his hand to me. I hesitantly took his hand, and he helped me up the next two steps.

"You fought valiantly," he said to me, as if there weren't a thousand people watching us. "I have accepted Alex's request and you are granted my protection," he stated casually.

Alex's request?

Lord Vertas continued to speak in a voice for all to hear. "I award you this medallion that you shall always have, to signify that you are the best this land has been blessed with." He placed the chain that the medallion was on around my neck as I tilted my head forward.

The silvery green medallion wasn't very big, maybe the size of a coin, but there was an intrinsic pattern carved in it. The design was black, giving the medallion an exotic appearance. When I glanced up, Phillip was standing behind Lord Vertas, smiling charmingly at me. I stared at Lord Vertas who was distracted for only a moment before his eyes shifted to mine.

"May I see the weapon that has helped aid you in this Tournament?"

"Of course," I said, but as I reached back to grab it, I remembered I never picked it up. I was suddenly very embarrassed. "I think, I think I left it on the… Alex must have picked it up," I stated, knowing that he wouldn't ever let me leave it behind. I searched the crowd at the bottom of the stairs, but Alex wasn't there. Where was he?

"Perhaps another time then," he said kindly, and I glanced back at him. "I do believe that I will be seeing you again," he continued, but I wasn't listening. Where was Alex? Lord Vertas had said that *Alex requested* I be given his protection. A tinge of worry moved through me as I searched the ocean of people for him.

Alex was gone? He left?! No, he wouldn't have left me today.

I was startled away from my search as Lord Vertas leaned in close to me, and whispered for only me to hear.

"I think that you should run."

203

As he moved his face slightly in front of mine, I saw his vivid green eyes that held the same wisdom that I had seen in Alex's.

He lifted his chin up and looked passed the Arena. Lord Vertas stood up straight, staring at me with curiosity for a moment. I had no idea what he meant, and I continued to search for Alex. He wasn't here. I quickly turned to Lord Vertas, who was still watching me.

I didn't care why he was, I was only concerned with where Alex went. I glanced back at the bottom of the stairs and anxiously at Lord Vertas. He stared at me with curiosity for a moment before he smiled, and turned to head back up the stairs as did Phillip. I was suddenly very alarmed about the notion that Alex had left.

"Now, for the winner of the Tournament…" Lord Vertas said as he began his speech for the winner.

I glanced back up to Lord Vertas …*you should run.*

I looked to the horizon out of habit, and fear grabbed me so tightly that I couldn't breathe. Alex, wouldn't…

I ran down the stairs the best I could, hearing everyone gasping in surprise, but I didn't pay attention to anyone. I continued to hobble hastily, passing everyone who had watched Phillip and I battle to be the winner, not caring about what they were saying.

I had to find Alex.

I didn't stop until I returned to our room. Alex wasn't here, and neither was Storm. Panic began to take its hold on me.

Lord Vertas said that he would accept Alex's request to protect me… I was having a hard time swallowing those words. It made it sound like Alex was leaving, for good. No, no, Alex wouldn't leave for good. He couldn't leave me. There had to be another explanation. I ran my hand through my hair as my fear of Alex leaving again became strong in my mind.

I suddenly felt like a little kid and wanted to cry. Alex was known for disappearing on a whim. As a child, there were a few times that I saw Storm racing for the horizon, I would chase the sunset to find him, but I never caught up.

I had to find him. I behaved so badly towards him today. It was because of him that I had been able to train for this Tournament, to be able to compete among the best of this land. I couldn't let him disappear thinking that I didn't appreciate all that he had done for me. What if he *never* returned?! That thought ripped through me.

I have accepted Alex's request and you are granted my protection.

Alex *was* leaving for good this time.

I limped quickly through town in the direction that Lord Vertas had motioned. As I exited the overcrowded town, I saw Storm and Alex walking slowly down the trail. Walking, not racing, but they were almost to the woods.

My heart panicked, he couldn't leave me! I ran as fast as I could, fighting off the fatigue that wanted me to collapse and the pain that burned horribly.

"Alex!" I yelled. "Alex!"

They entered the woods, but I was catching up. I searched for more strength. I had to reach him! I ran about a hundred feet stumbling my way through the forest when I finally saw that Alex had halted.

"Sonia, what are you doing?" he inquired as he stared at me in surprise, sliding off of Storm. "Why aren't you with Vertas? Are you okay?"

I stopped in front of him, "You can't leave me. I was so rude to you," I quickly said, collapsing towards the ground. His arms reached out and caught me. He pulled me close to him. I breathed in his scent, and clutched his arms tightly with my hands. He couldn't leave me!

"What are you talking…"

"I was so angry," I interrupted, "because I thought that you and Phillip, or you and Marty… that *you* wanted me to fail. I thought that you were so distant from me because I was winning and it wasn't what you wanted…"

"Sonia, I will always want for you what you want," he said. "I saw Phillip so close to you, saw him kiss you. I thought you were angry that I interrupted. He told me that…"

"He did that spitefully, he saw you coming… he said let the competition begin," I hastily informed him.

Alex couldn't leave… not just because I had behaved badly.

I gazed into his eyes that looked as though they were swimming with power.

Alex couldn't leave because...

His arm pulled me closer as he touched the side of my face with his other hand. I saw the conflict in his eyes. His arm started to release me and his hand began to slide away from my face.

"I watched you defeat man after man, there is nothing you desired more than to win," he stated. "Never once did you look to me today. You desire no one." He wasn't angry as he spoke, in fact he sounded like he was trying to convince himself.

"I didn't understand at the time. I..."

I stopped talking as I understood why I was in a panic.

Alex couldn't leave because I...

I quickly grabbed his shoulders, not allowing him move away from me. His eyes locked onto mine, and I felt like he was gazing into the depths of my soul.

...because I wanted him with me.

My heart began to race. How did I not notice before?

"Vertas will keep you safe. You need to..." he began, but stopped talking as I slid my hand around the back of his neck, and held myself closer to him.

I shook my head as I slowly moved my other hand to touch the other side of his face, and he closed his eyes. I took a deep breath, stood on my tiptoes, and moved my face closer to his until my lips touched his. As he began to kiss me, the butterflies

207

in my stomach burst into fire that raced through my entire body.

"It can't be me," he whispered as his lips moved away from mine. His hands let go of me and he moved away, leaning against a tree. He wasn't rejecting me. I could see there was something else.

"Alex," I softly said, cautiously moving closer to him again.

He focused on me with desire, but shook his head. "I can't... Lord Vertas..."

I shook my head, not understanding his words when I could see that he did want me. I stared into his eyes as I stood in front of him, debating what to do. He had always looked after me, protected me. He took a fragile, confused girl, and made me confident and strong. He had always been exactly what I needed to help me find my way.

I couldn't imagine my life without him as I grew up.

I couldn't justify that he didn't want me after that kiss, nor with the way that he was looking at me right now.

I couldn't imagine my life without him now.

I stepped closer and when he didn't move away, I closed my eyes. I caressed his cheek with mine until my lips were close to his ear.

And I couldn't imagine the rest of my life without him.

"It's you," I breathed out, "It's always been you."

His arms confidently came around me, as if him embracing me was always the way it should have been. My lips traveled along his jaw line.

"Sonia," he started.

"You can't leave me," my lips whispered. "I need you."

His arms tightened around me, holding me securely to him, and I heard him exhale deeply. His lips touched mine and I knew whatever had been holding him back was gone. There was strength and desire in his kiss, and I wanted more. I moved my body just far enough away to get his shirt off as quick as I could.

I ran my fingers over the warm smooth skin on his chest, over his shoulder, and onto his back. I felt him release the ties of my armor as though he'd done it a million times. His hands quickly slid under my shirt. The heat of his touch on my skin made my whole body quiver. I *needed* more of…

I was suddenly ripped away from him, and my body fell to the cold ground. I opened my eyes to see Alex's body hit a tree and fall to the ground.

"ALEX!!" I yelled as fear raced through me. I was on my feet in an instant, but someone's arms had captured me. I struggled to get free of the arms that held me. Alex wasn't getting up. I needed to get to him. I heard Storm neighing fiercely in the distance. I couldn't imagine what was going on until Marty and Phillip stepped between us.

I glared at them, and stomped on the foot of the man that held me. His grip loosened just enough that I could break free. I attempted to run passed Marty and his son. I avoided Phillip, but Marty got a hold of my arm and pulled me to him.

"It seems there is one thing more you and I disagree on," he snarled at me. He grabbed the medallion from around my neck and yanked it off of me, throwing it deep into the forest.

I punched Marty, but his grip didn't loosen, in fact he tightened his hold until I cried out in pain. "You are no longer going to be a part this life. No power can protect you now!" he growled. "Phillip!"

"Alex has warmed you up for me, I see," Phillip remarked from behind me.

I didn't pay any attention to him. I glanced at Alex's motionless body and Marty chuckled haughtily.

"He had his chance. How many years has he been in your pathetic life? Now, it's our turn."

"Don't worry, Sonia, I won't rush it," Phillip said as he stepped next to me.

I swung my arm and he caught it. He had a dagger in his other hand, and I fearfully glanced up at his face.

"It has to hurt or you wouldn't know that it really happened," Phillip said, but before he could bring the dagger closer to me I kicked it out of his hand and brought my heel into his knee. He let go of me, and in the next instant had I grabbed onto Marty's arm with my hand and swung him as I twisted myself around. I was actually able to shift him so that he was off balance. I quickly kicked at him and as he hit the ground, he let go of me.

I ran toward Alex again. Storm jumped over me and stopped as Marty roared angrily. Storm stared at me before he turned his attention to Marty, blowing a warning gust of air. I saw my sword in the bag that was packed on his back. I stepped forward, and grabbed its handle, sliding it into the sheath on my back.

Storm angrily whinnied as I turned back towards Alex. I heard Storm stomp the ground and make a strange noise, but I didn't look to see what was going on - all of my attention was on Alex. I quickly knelt down next to him, and I realized that he was still breathing. The dragon tattoo on his back seemed more vivid than the last time I had caught a glimpse of it. I rolled him over onto my lap and touched his face. He was burning up.

"Alex!" I yelled in panic.

"Storm get her out of here," he said in a stronger voice than I had expected as his eyes opened, and some of my panic disappeared. Storm stomped the ground again. Alex's eyes focused on me before he hastily sat up and abruptly moved away from me. "You have to get her to Vertas!" he growled. Storm made another strange sound, but I just stared at Alex.

"I'm not leaving without you," I said, trying to help him up.

"Sonia, you have to get away from me," he loudly said, almost hurtfully, and I stopped helping. He fell against a tree as he got to his feet and shook his head as though trying to clear his head.

Storm made a lot of noise, and then was at my side. I watched Alex fight to stand on his own. I tried to help again, but he stumbled a few steps away from me.

I heard the strange language in the back ground, and Alex glared behind me, but I didn't care about any of it. I was trying to understand what I did that was wrong. I had felt that he wanted me, I *knew* that he did.

Something sliced through my shoulder, and I stared at Alex helplessly before the pain registered. I saw the dagger that was now covered in my blood embedded in the tree behind him. Alex body tensed and I glimpsed at my shoulder to see that the dagger had cut through my loose armor. I glanced back up at Alex who was furiously staring at my shoulder.

"Get out of here!" he roared, without looking at me.

I didn't understand anything that was going on, except that I didn't want to be away from Alex.

Alex grabbed me around my waist, his hands burning on my sides as he lifted me onto Storm. He quickly tied my hands before putting the rope in Storm's mouth, so that I was practically hugging Storm. Alex growled in the language I didn't understand, and Storm took off running. I glanced behind me to see that Alex had moved between them and us.

Phillip was moving towards Alex, his face full of malice, while Marty was laughing in the background. I could have sworn that the eyes on Alex's tattoo were glowing with fire before the trees obscured my view.

"Turn around Storm, we have to go back!" I yelled when I could no longer see Alex.

I pulled against the rope that Alex used to tie me to Storm, but Storm refused to yield. Why wouldn't he turn around?! Did he not care about Alex?! Tears were racing down my face at the idea that Phillip and Marty were going to kill Alex.

Storm whinnied, bringing my attention to the other voices that were nearby. I looked forward as Storm halted, and saw Lord Vertas in front of the horse.

"John, go in there," he commanded, and John raced towards the woods that I wanted to return to.

Storm made some noise as I continued to struggle against the rope, refusing to give up the idea that I could get free.

"Her shoulder looks pretty bad. Come on Storm, let's get her to the castle."

"NO! Alex needs more than John to help him!" I exclaimed.

"Alex is the best our people have ever seen," Lord Vertas said. "He'll be fine."

The orange sun set, casting us in darkness. I knew I would be little help to Alex, but I continued to struggle to get free. I *needed* to be with him. Lord Vertas began to ride away, and Storm rode next to him.

"I can see why he tied you to Storm now," Lord Vertas said with surprise.

I didn't look at him. I continued to struggle against the ropes as I stared at the forest that was getting further away. I couldn't believe...

213

There was a bright ball of fire at the edge of the forest where we had been.

NO!! Tears began streaming down my face, and I stopped struggling. I had to get back there! I had to...

My whole body began to shut down. I fell against Storm's soft mane, feeling as though I had been fatally wounded.

"He's gone," I heard Lord Vertas say softly. "We need to hurry while we have the time."

I felt Storm begin to run faster. I didn't understand. Lord Vertas and Alex were friends. I thought... How could he be...

Suddenly it didn't matter. Nothing did.

END OF BOOK 1

Keep reading for a preview of :

(BOOK 2)

THE SHADOW DRAGON:
ALEKSERTAC

CHAPTER ONE

"Sonia, what has happened to you?"

It was my father's voice, but I didn't open my eyes to look at him. I didn't want to see him. I didn't want to see anyone.

"Please, look at me," he sadly said. "Lord Vertas sent for me. He seems very concerned about you. No one knows what is wrong with you."

So what.

"Krissy is sorry for all the things she's said to you before the Tournament, and that she didn't go to any of your matches. She doesn't understand what happened."

I didn't care.

"Lord Vertas has sent some people to help work the land, so you can just rest." He fell silent and his hand moved down the side of my face. "He says you may stay here indefinitely."

That doesn't bother you?

"Please look at me," he pleaded. "Give me some sign that you're alright. The Tournament has been over for almost four days. All of your wounds are healing. Lord Vertas has assured me that there isn't anything physically wrong with you, and yet you haven't..."

"Jack, may I have a word with you?" Lord Vertas asked in the distance.

"Of course, Lord Vertas," my father answered as footsteps walked over to where we were.

"I'm working hard to figure out what is ailing your daughter, and I have a theory. It doesn't make sense, but... May I ask you some questions?"

"Yes, of course, but I don't know that I'll have the answers."

"What was the relationship between Sonia and Alex?"

"Umm, she looked up to him, more than even me most days. He always seemed like her big brother as she grew up. He argued with her and protected her."

"And recently, did you notice anything *more* between them?"

"No, they have always interacted closely together," he informed Lord Vertas. "Her sister had accused them of being indecent, but Alex wasn't that guy. And even if he was, Sonia would have noticed and she would not have allowed it. All she wanted, all she ever wanted, was to be in that stupid Tournament."

"What happened after the incident in the Batwas Valley?"

"*You* know about that?" my father asked in surprise.

"Yes, information like that travels quickly. It is well known that she survived an encounter with the Ortal."

"Barely," my father whispered. "He brought her home from the Batwas Valley, and stayed to heal her. I had thought that meant he wanted to have her. Why else would he risk his life against the Ortal? He put so much time and energy into her recovery. He was determined to save her. The Ortal venom had progressed so far that I couldn't see how she'd survive, but Alex was not going to lose her. After all that effort, after saving my daughter from death, he deserved to have her. So I..."

"But he declined?" Lord Vertas interrupted in surprise.

"Said that she was out of his realm. I gave him every opportunity I could to change his mind, but he only wanted to train her."

"Really," Lord Vertas replied, sounding intrigued.

"I knew he could protect her, that she'd be safe with him - safer than with any man, including me."

"This is true. What about her? What was her interest?"

"Honestly, I don't think she knows that she's supposed to be with a man. That she's supposed to love a man, not compete against him. Her only focus since the last time Alex stayed with us has been that Tournament."

"You understand what has been going on... Marty, Phillip, the Ortal..." he paused a moment, but my father didn't say anything. "I thought that you might."

"She is like her mother," Father commented with mixed feelings. "That is why I didn't mind her being with Alex. No one is better trained with a sword than he. Her skill with a sword outshined the men in our town, but I did not want her in the Tournament."

"I watched her fight against John and Phillip. She, like her mother, is amazing," Lord Vertas agreed.

"I know," my father replied sadly. "But no one ever tried to kill Elizabeth."

My father's fingers brushed across my forehead.

"Why don't you come and eat," Lord Vertas suddenly said. "I insist. You've traveled a great distance to get here."

"I don't want to leave her alone."

"She won't be alone," a deep voice assured him.

"John will stay here. You don't have to worry, John is trustworthy."

I listened to them walk away from me. All that had been talked about was unimportant to me, and my mind drifted back to nothing.

***

The bright light that was all around me burned my eyes a little less today. I couldn't remember the last time I slept, or how many days had passed. My father came and went, but I wasn't keeping track of that either. I only knew that he was here or he wasn't.

Today, I decided that I didn't want to stare at the bright ceiling and I rolled onto my side. I was lying in a dark green, fluffy bed. I saw my hands in front of me. Both wrists were wrapped in white cloth. My injuries had been explained to me, as though I cared. The rope that Alex had used to tie my wrists had cut deeply into my skin from my struggling.

Alex...

I quickly shifted my eyes away from my wrists and stared at nothing, with no destination or focus in mind.

I found myself wishing that the Ortal had killed me, that the Shadow Dragon hadn't rescued me for Alex to find. Tears began to slide down my cheeks at the thought of Alex.

"Ahh, you've decided to come back to us," Lord Vertas commented kindly.

I didn't look towards the sound of his voice, nor did I blink, or give any sign that I had heard him. I didn't understand why I felt this way. I knew I wasn't injured, nor did I feel weak. I just didn't have the will to want to do anything. I wanted to believe it was because I had spent so much time training for the Tournament, and now it was over.

It was over, I didn't win, and Alex was... Alex was... gone.

I didn't feel this way when I lost to Phillip. I remembered my disappointment, but it was nothing compared to how I felt now. And my disappointment had been short lived... because of Alex. It was short lived because I realized that I *desired* Alex - that I needed him in my life.

The Tournament that I had trained so hard for suddenly meant nothing to me. I didn't care about proving myself to anyone, practicing my swordsmanship to protect myself and my family. It no longer mattered to me that I lost to Phillip, or that Marty had ripped my medallion from me. Without Alex, life no longer held any interest to me.

I closed my eyes against the tears that filled my eyes.

"You need to get up," Lord Vertas whispered.

After a moment I opened my eyes, staring at nothing until he moved into my line of sight. My eyes shifted to his handsome face to see him smiling kindly. His arms reached for me and sat me up. He moved my legs off the bed before he sat in front of me. He touched my face with one hand, his vibrant green eyes searching deep into mine until his smile disappeared. His hands didn't feel right touching me, causing an overwhelming sadness to sink into my heart. I started to slump back to the bed, but Lord Vertas quickly sat next to me to keep me sitting up.

"This is more complex than I had originally thought," he commented softly as tears moved down my cheeks again. I wasn't upset. It was like my eyes knew how sad my heart was and wept for it.

"John, go get Storm," Lord Vertas commanded as he turned his head. "We're going for a ride."

"But…" John began, sounding as though he was about to argue.

"I can't allow her to be like this any longer," Lord Vertas stated. "The matter needs to be dealt with."

I listened to John hurrying away. Lord Vertas touched my face with a gentleness that hadn't been in his voice just now. He pulled me close to him and lifted me out of the bed.

"Sir, John said you are leaving. Let me take her for…" a new voice started. "Right," the new voice said as though it were dumb to have suggested such an idea. "May I ask where you're going?"

"No."

"Will you need anything?"

"No," Lord Vertas stated with irritation, and the man remained quiet.

Lord Vertas carried me through the grand halls that Krissy would have drooled over. *If* there was any drool left from being in Lord Vertas' presence.

I focused on Lord Vertas' shirt, watching the light fade in and out. I imagined that there must be large windows lining this stretch of hallway because the light hardly faded before it became bright again. The light disappeared for several moments before the full strength of the sunlight fell upon us, causing my eyes to close.

A horse breathed out hard a short distance from us.

"Thank you, John," Lord Vertas said. "Would you mind riding with us?"

"Of course not," he happily replied. "Let me get Mac."

"Would you hold her for a moment?"

John didn't answer him.

"I promise he's not going to notice," Lord Vertas stated.

"He will notice. At the Tournament…"

"Fine, but he'll be too distracted to care."

John lifted me out of Lord Vertas' arms. It must have looked quite comical, me in John's arms.

The horse stomped his foot hard on the ground.

"It is not me," Lord Vertas stated. "Sonia's needs are beyond what Alex had asked of me."

The horse whinnied softly. I turned my head and glanced over at… Storm? There was no mistaking Storm, I just couldn't believe he was here. If Storm was here that meant that my worst nightmare was real, which caused a little more of me to disappear.

"Yes, I think so. You should have told me," Lord Vertas gently said, and Storm made an irritated noise. "He didn't?! Well, I need clarification. Will you allow us to ride you?"

Storm neighed fiercely, abruptly rearing and slamming his hooves on the ground.

"Look at her Storm," Lord Vertas loudly said, not sounding the least bit intimidated by Storm's show of anger and defiance. "Just this once. Victor will not allow her on him, and she will not hold on to you."

Storm moved over to John and I turned my head, closing my eyes. I was not Alex, and it was my fault that Storm was without him.

"Storm, you are the only one who can find him," Lord Vertas somberly remarked.

Storm's nose pressed against my face, and I opened my eyes. He whinnied softly as though he were telling me a secret before he neighed a little louder in Lord Vertas direction.

"Thank you," Lord Vertas humbly said.

John handed me back to Lord Vertas who was now on Storm's back. Lord Vertas cradled me on his lap, keeping me close to him. I heard another horse gallop next to us a few moments later, which I assumed was John and Mac.

"I don't think this is a good idea," John commented. "Taking her to…"

"This needs to be dealt with, or she will die anyway."

"But I thought he said…"

"He did, which is why *I* am taking her to him. Somehow a bond must have connected, and it's killing her spirit. He is the only one who will know how we can help her."

"He's going to be angry that we brought a mortal into the Ancient realm."

"I'll deal with him. Now, we must ride quickly to get passed the Dark Forces."

Lord Vertas spoke in the language that was now familiar, but I didn't understand. Storm breathed out stubbornly, and Lord Vertas continued to talk to him in a calm voice, but I could hear the urgency in his tone. After a few moments, Storm began running.

The wind raced passed me, and I knew we must be traveling at a faster pace than I ever had before. I continued to stare at the space between me and Lord Vertas' chest, not caring about what Lord Vertas had figured out or where he was taking me.

TITLES BY AMANDA SCHMIDT:

Taken: Marks of the Satrii

Taken Blades of the Ytinu Srebas (Book 2)

Solace: Uncharted Territory

Solace(Book 2): Lost

The Shadow Dragon: Orbs of Fire

The Shadow Dragon: Aleksertac (Book 2)

Not Human

Heart of the Emperor

CONNECT WITH ME ONLINE:

My blog:
http://amandaschmidt09.blogspot.com

Facebook:
https://www.facebook.com/AmandaSchimdtFans

Twitter:
http://twitter.com/@AmandaSchmidt09

Email:
aschimdtbooks@gmail.com

ABOUT THE AUTHOR:

Amanda Schmidt graduated from Eastern Michigan University and lives in Michigan with her family. When she's not being a mother of three she is out hiking or practicing Tai Chi, but most likely she is found with a book.

Amanda is a new and talented author who is able to take you into a world and captivate your attention. She beckons us to believe in dreams that allow us to think outside the box, and become more than we thought we could be.